Whiskey Tango Foxtrot

Divided We Fall

By W. J. Lundy

V7.24.2015.01

Whiskey Tango Foxtrot
Divided We Fall

© 2015 W. J. Lundy

Cover Design by Andres Vasquez Junior

Editing: Terri King, Sara Jones

This book is a work of fiction. The names, characters, places, and incidents are products of the writer's imagination or been used fictitiously and are not to be construed as real. Some places, especially military locations and facilities are intentionally vague or incorrect in layout and security perimeter. Any resemblance to persons, living or dead, actual events, locales, or organizations is entirely coincidental. All Rights Are Reserved. No part of this book may be used or reproduced in any manner whatsoever without written permission from the author.

* * *

Dedicated to the American Warfighter.

"Then join hand in hand, brave Americans all! By uniting we stand, by dividing we fall!" John Dickinson, July 1768

PROLOGUE

The nightmare woke him from his sleep; the sound of his own screams as he called out his wife's name... always her name. He turned in the bed to search for his smart phone. It no longer worked, not for making calls anyway, but he still used it to check the time and keep track of his notes... to see the photos of his girls, read old messages from her. Finding it tucked underneath him, he pushed a button and lit its display—*02:30*. He had only slept for an hour. He reached for the nightstand and turned on the touch-activated lamp, filling the room with a warm light. Looking at the other bunks, he could see that he was still alone. No one else checked into the lonely hotel hundreds of feet under the rock.

He had fallen asleep on top of the bedding, still in his uniform, having only taken off his shoes and jacket before sleep found him. He moved to an upright position and sat drearily, staring at the floor. He felt far older than his forty-two years. The months and days without sunlight were taking a toll on him—the chaos and the moving, the running, and of course, the fighting. The thought of it all caused him to steal a quick glance at the Glock in the shoulder holster resting over the back of a chair near his bed.

A strobe light began flashing above the door. He'd become familiar with the light. It'd been going off almost constantly since they'd arrived at the bunker complex in Colorado. It meant they were at the blast doors… survivors, infected, attackers… who knew? It didn't make much difference to the security teams. The first move against the steel bunker doors had been by locals. Not criminals, not militias, not even the hate groups; mostly just average civilians—now refugees in their own country. The bunker was not a secret in the nearby town. Secrets were hard to keep these days. After the breakup of the Soviet Union, this bunker became common knowledge; a television documentary had even featured the site years earlier.

When the barricades broke and the roadblocks failed, hundreds, then thousands, of civilians made their way up the mountain pass. They occupied the road, pounding on the doors and begging for refuge. The Air Force provided as much assistance to them as they could; food drops had been made and they set up tents to try to shelter them. They even allowed some inside… those with special skills like doctors and engineers. The overall situation considered manageable, the approach road to the bunker converted into a survivors' camp.

That all changed when the first sightings of the infected reached the base of the mountain though. The bunker's command team ordered in all available air assets and even sent some of the security teams out beyond the perimeter to assist the state troopers. Holding the pass turned out to be impossible for the under-equipped law enforcement types. Wave after wave of them poured into the valley. Air National Guard combat planes provided close-air support, dumping everything onto the approaching enemy, but for every one killed, ten more of them were drawn into the valley.

The people at the bunker entrance began to panic as the sounds of the fight drew closer. Civilians rushed the outer fences and pushed through the gates; most of the security guards refused to fire on families — families looking for nothing but safety for their children. Several civilians managed to make it past the blast doors before the automated triggers closed and sealed them. Still, thousands more had not. The military inside all sympathized with the refugees. So many of the soldiers had no idea where their own families were, and they could not help but wonder if they were in the crowd beyond the heavy blast doors.

He stood in the control room when the infected finally broke through the final defenses. The guards used spotlights to try to blind them and slow their advance. It did not work; the Primals — as they would come to call them — found their way through and made their way up the mountain. The external closed-circuit cameras captured everything. Pockets of soldiers who held the lines outside — refusing orders to fall back to the bunker — chose to make a last stand in front of the civilians and formed a meager perimeter around the survivors.

The colonel watched, terrified, as state troopers and security guards came crashing through the woods ahead of the advancing monsters and ran through the crowd of civilians in a fast retreat. Shouting warnings to run, they caused further panic in the crowds. Realizing early on that the bunker's gates were never going to be open to them, some ran beyond it and farther up the mountain. The remaining civilians pushed themselves against the doors, crushing each other under their own weight.

The enemy calls started; distant at first, but soon the high-pitched screams were so loud they drowned out the outside speakers. Loose pockets of armed men tried to fight; they stood their ground but were quickly overwhelmed. The Primals flooded their simple defense and mixed in with the civilians, slashing and attacking everything. The rage-filled figures cut through flesh with dulled teeth. Amongst the chaos, his eyes focused on a lone Marine who fired his rifle directly into the charging mass. When his weapon failed, without hesitation, he jumped the barrier and used his rifle as a club. The Marine knocked one down with a blow to the head then used a KA-BAR to take out another. Soon the Marine disappeared in a massing flurry of bodies.

The colonel turned away from the video feed, refusing to watch anymore. He spun his chair toward a wall and prayed for his own family in Virginia. He had lost contact with them after the first of the barricades and safeguards were in place. Now he second-guessed himself constantly for not breaking his orders and going to his family. What kind of father does not put his family first? He had abandoned them in their greatest time of need. His last contact with his wife was a simple text message: orange—a prearranged code word signaling her to gather everything and head to his father's house in West Virginia. He never received a reply.

After 9/11 and his posting to the Pentagon, his clearance elevated and he became privy to the threats the world really faced. He discussed contingency plans with his wife, and they developed a strategy to get her and the kids quickly out of the area in case of an emergency. Different words for different directions or contingencies: black, lock the doors and go to the basement; orange, head for the mountains; blue, meet at a storage building near the coast; white, drive west and stop for no one. They kept a bag packed on a shelf in the garage and a safe with a loaded pistol in the trunk of the SUV. He programmed rural routes into the vehicle's GPS, avoiding the interstates under each color. She should have easily made it to his father's home outside the city limits, far off the grid and located in the high country. They would be safe there, he reassured himself, because most of the attacks were against cities or high-population areas.

She knew he would find his way there as soon as he could after things died down or once they contained it. He had hoped that when everything settled, he would somehow be able to leave for a couple days and check in on them. However, things never died down; instead, they escalated. Defensive lines and cities fell, the borders sealed, air traffic froze, and highways closed or were congested beyond use. Nobody knew how to fight this enemy. The government reacted slowly to the early reports. Small attacks—probes of two and three against rural locations or on terminals at airports; crazed men and women who came out of nowhere and attacked without mercy—soulless faces that showed no remorse in their killing, never halting their attack. State governments began to clash with the decision making of the President. Most of the federal troops abandoned their posts, and everything quickly fell into chaos. Without troops to hold back the waves and organize the withdrawal, everything spiraled out of control.

The Pentagon was surrounded by remnants of the old guard in a final defense when he had been ordered to leave. He could hear the fighting from his office deep inside the building when an Air Force sergeant burst through his door and handed him a shoulder holster containing a Glock. He took a family photo from a picture frame and folded it into his wallet before following the sergeant into the hallway. With the outer rings of the building compromised, parts of the Pentagon had been intentionally set ablaze to slow the Primals' advance. All was lost and the defensive operation became an evacuation.

All essential personnel moved to the large courtyard in the center of the Pentagon. The defenders prepared final protective lines. Guards desperately used C4 and detonation cord to knock down trees and create a landing zone for the swarms of aircraft orbiting overhead. Escorted by soldiers, he rushed through the maze of barricades and quickly boarded a USN SH-3 helicopter. With little fanfare, a crewmember pushed him into a seat and closed the door. As the helicopter climbed into the air, he could see the tracer rounds zip across the courtyard as the things broke through the south side. His helicopter climbed higher into the dark clouds of black smoke, and he lost site of the building below him.

He strained to see out of a portside window. The capital below swarmed in flames as people cowered in the streets. On the National Mall, armored vehicles sat stoically at barricades with guns thumping, trying to hold back the waves of attackers. Twisting streams of tracers arced down city streets and into apartment buildings. His mind could not process the sight before him. The briefings described the chaos outside — the troops on the ground had dubbed it the Meat Grinder — but seeing it was far worse. As the SH-3 helicopter joined an aerial convoy of several others of varying makes, civilian and military alike, he lost sight of the burning city below.

The strobe light mounted above his door stopped flashing, pulling him from his thoughts. He quickly put on his shoes and stood facing the mirror; he saw a face that he had not shaved in days and gray, matted hair in need of a cut. The dark circles resting under his eyes made him look as if he lost a fight with a very big stick. Shaking off the feelings of despair, he slipped on the shoulder holster and put on his jacket. He began to move toward the door when it pulled out and away from him. A uniformed enlisted man burst through the threshold then stopped, looking startled to see him dressed and on his feet.

"Sorry to disturb you, Colonel Cloud; General Reynolds is asking for you."

CHAPTER 1
Combat Outpost Savannah

"Winter is on us."

"Yeah," Brad answered, not looking back. Standing at the farthest end of the outpost, high in the south-facing tower, he could see beyond the cleared fields of fire and into the abandoned homes of Savannah. He looked down the rows of empty streets at abandoned cars and overgrown yards. Occasionally, a Primal would move out of cover but just as quickly vanish into the shadows. The things had become aware. Like any apex predator, they started to adapt to the food chain and their local environment. They would still venture near the outpost, attacking patrols outside the wire, even massing when they detected weakness, but normally staying out of range of the outpost's towers and guarded gates during daylight hours.

The constant threat made life within the camp grueling, especially on the many civilians and families inside, not used to the high-tempo lifestyle. The Primals were still deadly and would often make probing attacks against soft spots under the cover of darkness, occasionally breaking through the defenses and sometimes even managing to find themselves inside the camp. These attacks were always shut down quickly with a well-disciplined guard force. Still, the nocturnal pack hunters were unpredictable in the size and shape of their assaults and forced the camp to maintain a grueling state of readiness.

Rigid steel and concrete walls, braced up with compacted soil, ringed the Savannah outpost. Evenly spaced along the outpost's perimeter were tall watchtowers. At one time, they all were occupied and often still were in times of emergency or heavy Primal activity. Currently, the only areas manned around the clock were the towers in strategic positions — along highways, gates, or in certain areas of overwatch. Roving guards heavily patrolled the areas between the towers and other void areas, checking for breaks in the wire or other indications of a Primal attack.

Brad and Brooks had begun making a habit of running the trail that ran along the inside of the post's perimeter every morning. Often they would stop at one of the abandoned towers and use the high vantage points to learn the lay of the land. Brooks made diligent notes, logging avenues of escape and the best areas of defense in case they were overrun or had to bug out in a hurry. He kept his hand-drawn maps in a fanny pack he wore on his hip. He took inventory of the emergency provisions stored in every tower they visited.

Not looking up from the sketching on his map, Brooks said, "You know it won't be easy."

"What in the last few months has been easy?" Brad responded. He walked away from the tower window and plopped into an old office chair. "The Rangers said we can use one of the birds to get back to Sumter—"

"And then what? You gonna walk all the way back to the 'stan?" Brooks asked.

Brad tossed an empty water bottle at the wall and stood. "What are we supposed to do? Leave them out there?"

Brooks shook his head and got to his feet. Grabbing his MP5, he slung it so that it hung over his back and prepared for the final leg of their run. "I'm just saying, we lost a lot of good people to get this far. How do we know they ain't better off where they're at?"

Brad stared far into the distance and pointed at a dark column of smoke climbing above a distant patch of green forest. "How long's that been there?"

"Started this morning," Brooks said. "Boys are saying an electrical storm started it; gets any bigger, could be a problem for us."

Brad moved closer to the open side of the tower while looking intently at the smoke on the horizon. "Damn, if the wind is just right, that would burn right up to the walls."

"Yup, and anything of value in the city, starve us all out," Brooks said.

Adjusting his shoulder holster, Brad pulled his sweatshirt down tight around his waist and moved to the ladder. "Could get out of control really fast…"

"You want to check it out? We could get a vehicle from the motor pool. I'm bored to death locked in garrison, anyway," Brooks said.

Brad grinned; the garrison life—threats or not—had become a bore, even though it allowed his injuries to heal. He wanted to get back outside to do his job, not post maintenance. The Rangers allowed them to leave the outpost on their downtime, but for the most part kept them assigned to limited duties and work parties, without allowing them on the daily combat patrols. He stopped and looked back at Brooks, speaking as he climbed down the ladder. "Let's go."

     At the bottom, Brad turned and ran across the post instead of following the path. The outpost contained all of Hunter Airfield, forest, and open ground. The old post fences, raised and reinforced, and areas of only chain link fence pushed back to meet highways or other natural barriers. The outpost was now completely self-contained, with more than enough room for the camp's inhabitants. The post walls were a priority, and everyone spent a fair share of time on the daily work parties that improved them.

Brad briefly looked back to see Brooks reach the bottom and begin to follow him. Brad picked up his own pace to try to stay ahead. He turned onto a narrow trail leading to the barracks, nodding to a pair of armed soldiers guarding the gate as he passed. Brad and the team could have taken their choice of any of the vacant homes located in the housing areas; instead, they chose to live in the large barracks building located near the center of the outpost. Not only to remind them that their situation was not permanent, but also to remain close to one another.

He slowed at the barracks building, which were three stories tall and surrounded by uncut grass. Boards covered the first floor windows and a thick coil of razor wire wrapped around the building's foundation. Not only did they secure the outer perimeter of the outpost, there were several areas within also covered and divided by fences. Each inhabited building was barricaded and secured by another pair of soldiers, who stood watch on the stoop of the barracks' entrance.

Brad eased into a jog then a walk as he turned to wait for Brooks. He grinned as he watched his friend pass onto the concrete walkway and move forward to meet him.

"You're getting faster, Army," Brooks said.

"Bro, I think you're getting slower—"

The door at the top of the steps leading into the barracks flew open, slamming against the handrail. The guards on the stoop quickly separated to make room for a group of soldiers in full kit rushing out. Brad reached out and grabbed a private. "What's the hurry?"

"There's a fire. Somewhere out past the city limits; sending out a patrol to check it out," the private said.

Brooks looked at Brad and smiled, shrugging his shoulders, and then turned to face the soldier. "Could you all use a couple extra hands?"

The private pulled away, trying to catch up with the others, and then looked back at Brad. "I'm sure the LT wouldn't turn down the help, but you better hurry; we're rolling in five mikes."

The young soldier ran down the path, eager not to be left behind. "We're on the way; tell them not to leave without us!" Brad shouted.

Chapter 2

Hairatan Customs Compound: Northern Afghanistan.

The soldier ran across the roof of the building, barely stopping in time before nearly tumbling down the open hatch and into the warehouse below. He caught himself and grabbed the rungs of the ladder. Gripping the side rails, he quickly slid to the bottom where the warehouse was tightly organized into individual living spaces. Fires smoldered in small metal rings, leaving a smoky scent in the cold dawn air. Most of the families had already reported for their daily work chores and the warehouse floor was empty except for a few women minding after small children who stopped and looked up at him, startled by his quick movements.

Making a quick dash for the large overhead doors, the soldier nodded his head apologetically and ran through the maze of blankets and bedding that covered the floor. He stopped for just long enough to survey his surroundings before continuing toward the guardhouse, quickly crossing the distance, and charging through the entrance. Heavy drapes and scraps of cardboard covered the windows, but the lanterns were still out; the nightshift guard force was not awake yet.

"Sergeant Turner!" he yelled as he moved through the narrow building, tripping and bumping into cots as he worked his way to the back in the dark. "Sergeant Turner!"

Startled awake, men rolled over in their bunks; some shouted obscenities while others pulled blankets over their heads. Turner sat up in his bed and looked at the excited soldier. "What the hell do you want, Mendez?" he said.

The soldier stopped just in front of Turner's rack, gasping to catch his breath. "Sorry… to wake you, Sergeant… but… the drone… the drone is back… and we think it might have dropped something."

His words suddenly caught the attention of the other men in the barracks, and Turner looked at the messenger wide eyed. "Dammit, get the scouts formed up and meet me by the vehicle gate. Hot damn, boys, this might be our lucky day!" Turner shouted. The bearded sergeant reached down and quickly pulled on his multi cam trousers and a thick thermal shirt. "Mendez! Hold up… how long has it been since you saw it?"

Mendez, who had already taken off toward the exit to gather the scouts, stopped and looked back. "We just spotted it, Sergeant; it looks like it dropped something in the container yard. Some sorta tube with a long streamer attached."

"Good, get moving. I'm right behind you."

Turner stood and stretched. He reached to a windowsill, grabbed at his green standard-issue canteen, and took a long pull of the cold water. Winter was nearing the compound and the temperature was dropping overnight. Soon, snow would come and the river would freeze. Survival of the camp was not in question, not from the weather, anyway; the Afghan people would make sure they lived through the winter—the problem was the Primals.

If the river froze, the hordes of crazies from the northern bank and the more populated city of Teremez would be able to cross. It was a constant concern to Turner since the first frost dropped over the compound a week ago. Maybe the drone would be the saving grace he'd been hoping for.

Turner strapped on his pistol belt then slung a rifle over his shoulder as he moved through the barracks toward the door. He stepped into the brisk air, squinting as his eyes adjusted to the bright sunlight. Despite the distance, he could see that soldiers in varying uniforms were grouping together at the main gate, making ready for a patrol. An Afghan scout walked among them, checking equipment and weapons. Turner reached into his shirt pocket and removed a half-smoked, hand-rolled cigarette. He placed it in his mouth and used a Zippo to light it.

Inhaling deeply, he closed his eyes, held in the smoke, and rolled his shoulders before exhaling. Turner stepped off toward the gate. As he moved, he watched the gathered men look at him; Mendez, with an Afghan scout close in tow, joined him halfway. The Afghan scout wore his traditional clothing of a dark wool sweater and cap. His beard was thick and his bushy hair pulled pack and tied. Close to his chest, he carried a collapsible AK74 with a hand-built suppressor.

"Morning, Hassan," Turner said, greeting the scout as they met on the path. "Are we ready?"

Hassan had earned his place on the base, quickly becoming one of his most dependable scouts. After the initial attack and fight for common survival became apparent, the differences between them, created by wars, quickly vanished. Hassan returned to the compound shortly after Sergeant Thompson departed with the SEALs, telling their story and promise for a rescue. The scout brought in more survivors he'd gathered on his journey and was always roaming the nearby villages in hopes of finding more.

"Yes, the men are ready. We can depart at your discretion," Hassan said.

"Primal activity?" Turner asked, looking at Mendez this time.

"No, Sergeant, the drone didn't seem to move them. The Primals still seem to be sticking to the city side… and of course them ones across the river. The yard is clear," Mendez said.

"Roger that. Send a runner to let the lookouts know we're entering the rail yard. "

Mendez turned on the balls of his feet to look at another soldier, who had been listening close by. Mendez nodded and the soldier took off toward the positioned guard towers.

Turner held up his rifle and chambered a round. "Alright then, move 'em out."

Mendez raised a hand and pointed at the gate. Two guards undid the latch and pulled it open just enough for a single man to exit through it. Hassan passed by the rest of the scouts as they formed into a column, their rifles unslung and held at the ready. Hassan was the first to pass through the gate and into the rail yard. The rest of the men moved out after him, keeping the formation tight. No need to spread out, as the Primals never attacked with grenades or explosives.

After moving fifty meters, Hassan left the blacktop road and stepped into the stacks of shipping containers. In the last months, the men of the compound completely walled in the camp with tall, fortified walls. Slowly, they enlarged the camp's perimeter, trying to expand the wire and clear their safe areas. Technically, the rail yard was now in what they called a "green zone" completely enclosed by wire, but they never left the gates without being on full alert.

Hassan slowly patrolled forward, carefully clearing every corner as he moved. The rest of the men kept pace; another Afghan scout stayed close behind Hassan, and three soldiers with Turner closed up the rear. Most of the locks on the shipping containers were cut, the goods long ago inventoried and taken inside the main gates for safekeeping. Hassan stopped often to look at the ground to check for trails or the wires and engineer tape tied between the aisles to help identify if an intruder had slipped in.

They moved further in, around corners, and toward the center of the container holding yard. Hassan dropped to a knee, looked back at Turner, and tapped where a shirt collar would be if he had worn one. Turner nodded and moved to the front of the column and knelt next to Hassan.

Hassan pointed in the distance at an olive green, pill-shaped device with at least fifty feet of bright metallic streamer trailing behind it. "I believe this is your item," he said.

Turner looked in the direction Hassan was pointing. Lifting his M4 to use the optics, he swept left and right before saying to Hassan, "Okay, let's move up." Turner then looked back at the rest of them and ordered, "Okay… you men get me a 360 security on this location."

Turner reached out and slapped Hassan on the back. "Okay, take me to it."

Hassan slowly moved back to his feet and crossed the open ground toward the olive green cylinder. All the while, the rest of the men spread out and circled the object, creating a full bubble of security as instructed. The cylinder was metallic with heavy foam rubber cushions on both ends. A ring at the back connected it to the streamer. Hassan grabbed the object and pulled it flat, then rolled it over.

"Well, I guess it's not gonna explode," Turner said.

Hassan nodded. He then reached down and, using a small dagger, tapped the cylinder. "It's hollow."

"Can you open it?" Turner asked.

Hassan turned the object over, examining both ends. He gripped the heavy foam rubber cap and peeled it back until it popped off with an audible snap. Exposed at the tip was a small seam and a yellow arrow painted around the lip, indicating the direction to turn. Hassan paused to look back at Tuner before gripping the cylinder between his knees and twisting at the top. Quickly rewarded with the spinning of the cap, he spun it several rotations then it dropped off. Hassan reached into the tube and pulled at a thick nylon rope, removing a foam, black, egg-shaped object that split open as soon as it left the throat of the cylinder.

"I've seen this before," Hassan said and smiled as he reached into the foam egg casing and removed the iridium satellite phone.

Chapter 3

Cloud followed the airman down the dimly lit corridors; the dampness of the hall affected his sinuses and the cold sent aches through his tired body. With nearly everything powered off to conserve energy, there was only enough ambient light to see the floor and bits of the walls. The deep mountain bunker was beginning to feel more like a tomb than a sanctuary.

Allowing the escort to stay just ahead of him, Cloud turned a corner and followed the airman through an open blast door. There were no other guards on duty in the lower chambers—not anymore. Everyone had moved to the upper levels now. Most programs had ceased; there was no longer a reason to keep the lower decks staffed. Security this low on the operations deck was limited to the elevators and access shafts. The corridors were silent other than the white noise created by the whirring of the ventilation fans; nevertheless, it still allowed their footsteps to echo off the walls hauntingly as they moved.

The escort stopped at an alcove and touched a glowing green-lit keypad before quickly entering a series of numbers. The door clicked with an electric buzz then the airman reached for a handle and pulled it open. Cloud followed him into a tight four-foot by eight-foot chamber, at the end of which stood another steel door with a camera mounted above it. Cloud stepped forward so that he was side by side with the escort and looked up at the camera. A red light mounted in the center of the door moved to green and the door slid open with a burst of air as the positive pressure leaked out. Cloud moved through the door and into a brightly lit command center.

"Colonel, if you need me I'll be up front," the airman said.

Embarrassed at having to be escorted, Cloud sheepishly nodded his reply. He moved out ahead of the escort to enter the great room, passing by empty workstations and cubicles; outdated charts and old bulletins covered the walls. Large monitors hung in a neat row—most powered off, others showing old situation maps or satellite photographs. As the crisis escalated and the situation deteriorated out of control, most of the staff were relieved or reassigned to other parts of the bunker. When the world went dark, there was nothing for most of them to do, nothing left to track.

At the end of the long row, the few remaining operators sat weary eyed, staring at flat screens as they scrolled through endless satellite images or reviewed week-old reconnaissance reports from the field. Cloud moved beyond them and entered a brightly lit, glass cutout room embedded into the corner of the chamber. A mahogany table surrounded by leather chairs took up most of the floor space, the outside walls were also covered with charts, a small table in a corner held a coffee pot, and a box on the floor sat, filled with brown MRE packages.

A man in dress uniform with General's Stars on his shoulders sat at the end of the table, reading a report; he looked up, acknowledging Cloud as he entered. "How'd you sleep, James? Coffee is fresh, if you want some."

"Thanks; slept like shit as usual," Cloud said as he walked to the small table and lifted a cup, blowing grime from the bottom and using a rag to wipe it clean. He flipped a toggle and filled the cup with the steaming hot liquid. Cloud took a sip that burnt his lip then moved to the end of the table to join the man. He pulled out a chair, sat, and then looked at the older man. The general dropped the report and slid it across the table to Cloud.

Cloud lifted the single sheet of paper and began reading. "This the current lab result? So what's with the strobe?" Cloud asked.

General Reynolds took a sip of his own coffee before leaning back in his chair. "Just one of the teams returning; all is secure, clean entry."

"Good to hear. So I'm guessing you didn't bring me down here for coffee."

Reynolds set his cup on the table and spun to look out the glass panels into the control room. He then turned back to Cloud and pointed at the page on the table. "We're getting nowhere with Aziz. We need the sample… I want that girl."

"Well… unless we want to go to war with a regiment of Rangers, I don't think it's going to happen anytime soon. Did you try contacting Colonel Ericson? He's a reasonable man."

"Of course I tried. He's not budging. Your boys from the sandbox have fed him a line of bull. He's holding her tight… says we're welcome to assist, but he's not giving up the girl."

"Can't blame him for that. I mean, we did leave his entire regiment out of the evacuation plans… left them out there to die." Cloud finished reading over the laboratory report and handed it back to the general.

Reynolds shook his head and forced a dry laugh. "I don't think the bastard trusts us. I'm still working another angle with the response teams, but in the meantime, I need you to pursue this other option—the leverage—just in case. That is why I sent for you."

Reynolds reached for a folder and removed a black-and-white overhead satellite image of the Hairatan customs compound. Cloud was familiar with the image and knew what it meant. "The phone's been delivered. Predator dropped it this morning. We have a C-17 on standby, ready to go; I just need you to convince them to get on it."

"Why wouldn't they? We're bringing them home."

"James, that's not all. I need to ask you. Do you think it'll be enough to convince them to give us the sample? Will they exchange the girl for these men? This isn't a cheap operation."

Cloud leaned back in his chair and squeezed his hands together, contemplating the question. "I think so. That team that captured Aziz... they're the real deal. If he thinks his men are at risk, and we can guarantee the girl's safety," Cloud paused and stared down at the photo, "then yes, they'll make the trade—with assurances, of course."

Reynolds sat up and looked directly at Cloud. "Assurances? Even for the sample... with everything that's at stake? James, if you can't pull this off, a lot of people will die."

Cloud raised his head, leaning toward the general. "Sir, it doesn't have to come to that. I can make it work. Colonel Erickson does not have the science to synthesize a vaccine from the girl, and they know it. We are the only hope any of them have for a cure. These men aren't a trade; they are the reward for doing the right thing." James turned in his chair, dropping his head again. "There's another option; we could do the right thing. Send a team to Savannah, work together, let them help synthesize—"

"Dammit, James! We've been over all of this before; it isn't up for discussion. Get them to give up the girl, or we'll take her. The unity of the nation is at stake."

The general stood and walked toward the glass, looking out over the command center floor. "The right thing," he said then turned and leaned against the back wall. "Speaking of the right thing, James, I saw the utilization report. You hijacked our keyholes to do some private browsing."

James frowned and his back involuntarily stiffened in the chair. "It was only briefly, sir, and I ordered them repositioned as soon as I finished."

"You do understand that the satellite assets are extremely limited. You can't be taking them off line for personal use."

Cloud shook his head and looked down at his folded hands. "Sir, if you'd just give me a team, I could get my family out of there. Then we don't need to have these discussions."

"James, do you know how many people we have in this facility and how many of those still have families out there, families that are missing?"

"Then hell, sir, let's get them all; we're only at forty percent capacity, and more deserting by the day. Get the names and locations… I'll start a priority list and let's get them. It would have a positive impact on morale."

"Sorry, James, it doesn't work that way. We would lose control of this place if we tried. Half these men would go mad if we went after their families and confirmed their worst fears. You know that over three-quarters of those family members are dead. You just need to take comfort in the fact that your girls are safe."

"For now they are." Cloud got to his feet and used a rag to wipe out the coffee cup; he moved to the end of the room and set it back on the tray. "If you need me, I'll be arranging the recovery of your leverage."

Chapter 4

He rushed forward, tripping and crashing through boxes of spoiled produce, crates of rotten tomatoes, and wilted lettuce. The pungent stench coated his shirt and pants, mixing with the sticky blood and mud. Joe-Mac crawled ahead then stumbled to his feet; he heard them running down the aisle in pursuit just behind him. Spinning back to his front, he nearly tumbled into a maggot-infested meat counter.

Repulsed and fighting the urges to vomit while ignoring the spasms in his back and stomach, he pressed forward, gasping for air. Each breath took in the stench of death and decay. He spotted stainless steel double doors set into the back wall. Joe dropped his shoulder and lunged through, breaking into an outer storage area. Light cut in from the rear, and he continued running, gaining distance on the sounds of those hunting him.

There was another door — gray steel with a push bar. Joe hit it hard and found himself in the bright light of a fenced-in loading dock. A chain secured the closed gates and barbed wire ran along the top of the fence. Joe heard the charging mob inside closing in on him; he pushed back, shoving the door hard. Next to him was a reel of fire hose and Joe grabbed at it. Unwinding as fast as he could, he wrapped the door's handle with the heavy hose and tied it shut just as the first of the infected monsters collided with it.

The hose pulled tight, but held. The door pushed open just enough for Joe to see the faces of the infected as they attempted to squeeze out. He reached for his hip; his pistol was gone, as was his machete, lost somewhere in the market. He was unarmed and alone. Nobody would know where he was… nobody would be coming for him.

Joe-Mac stepped away from the building to examine its shape and size, looking for a way out. Conduit with U-shaped brackets bolted in every few feet ran vertically on the outside walls all the way to the roof. With just enough of a gap that he could wrap his hands around them, he grabbed the gray plastic pipes, pulled hard, and found them tightly secured to the block wall.

More of the infected were gathering at the chain link fences behind him; the mass began pushing against it, causing the poles to lean inward. Joe-Mac reached up, gripped the conduit, and began shimmying up the side of the building. He scaled the building as fast as he could, pulling up his feet and pinching tight before reaching up, one hand at a time, then pulling himself up again.

His arms shaking, he reached the top ledge and pulled himself onto the roof. He rolled over the short knee wall, dropped to the asphalt coating, and lay on his back catching his breath while listening to the things below. Looking up at the blue sky, Joe-Mac clenched his eyes shut tight and said, "Why didn't I let them talk me out of this?"

His bag and belongings were all below and inside, far from reach — somewhere between the supermarket's pharmacy and produce section. He sure as hell wouldn't be going back for them. Not without an army. Where did they all come from? He was doing fine until he turned on his light; then they were everywhere, swarming in from out of the dark.

Joe shook his head and sat up, not wanting to think about what could've happened.

"You messed up good today, boy," he said.

Joe-Mac got to his feet and moved across the roof, back to the street side. The supermarket parking lot was empty except for a few burned-out cars and rusted shopping carts. Across the street was a mom-and-pop sporting goods store and next to that, an auto parts store. The gas station on the corner was nothing more than a burned-out hulk. The village of Seneca, West Virginia, had seen better days.

He was alone on a roof in the middle of nowhere… an all too familiar feeling. Loneliness didn't bother him. He'd lived a solitary life after leaving high school and most of his childhood life behind. Divorced parents in different cities. A few girls in far-off towns. No real career aspirations to speak of, he took odd jobs to pay for gas, working on construction sites or as a farmhand. He thought he'd have to grow up one day, but the apocalypse changed all of that.

Joe moved to the far corner of the building. He spotted his pickup truck where he'd left it at the far edge of the lot, tucked in behind overgrown shrubs. The area was clear, all of the infected having moved to the back of the store. He needed to leave.

Joe could still hear them pounding against the fence and the fire door. With no time to waste and not wanting to find himself trapped outside after dark, he decided to make his move. He pulled himself over the front of the store's face and hung so that his arms were fully extended then dropped to the fiberglass awning below. He hit hard and slipped on the surface made slick by weeks of mildew and decaying leaves, which coated the awning with slime. Before he could grab on to something solid, he began sliding and felt himself falling over the edge.

He thumped against the pavement, seeing stars as the wind left his body. Joe-Mac lay motionless, silently taking inventory of his body and listening to the surroundings. He was alone, nothing felt broken. He rolled to his belly and pushed up to his knees. Joe-Mac saw the truck, only a couple hundred yards away. He could easily make it—just get up and go.

"No," he said.

Joe-Mac didn't want to return to the cabin empty-handed, especially without the meds for Dan's granddaughter. He didn't need much, just something for the fever; aspirin would work, but antibiotics would be better. Joe promised the man he'd get them, and he didn't like to break promises.

He could see the sporting goods store, the front glass broken and the door kicked in. The shop used to have racks for long guns and a case full of pistols. That would all be gone now. Maybe he could find some camping gear... anything to make up for losing his pack and weapons. Joe took another quick look in both directions and stepped off toward the store.

The way was clear. The sunlight shone brightly; he thought that would keep most of them indoors. Joe looked back over his shoulder at the supermarket. "Yeah, they're all in there," he said. "I'll be all right."

Joe picked up a quick pace, nearly a jog, not wanting to be caught in the open. He crossed the street quickly and stopped along the brick wall of the storefront. Keeping his back to the wall, he moved to the edge of the window and peeked inside the building. Just as he had suspected, the weapons racks were bare; shelves once heavily stocked with ammunition, now cleared out. The glass countertop and gun case were broken and swept clean. In the back, he could still see shelves; covered in shadows, they may still hold something. He had to try.

Joe crouched low and moved into the doorway. He grabbed the edge of the wooden door and tried to push it closed. It swung easily, but the frame was twisted and the door refused to latch. Looking out, he spotted the infected moving back to the front lot. Several wandered between him and his truck. He desperately needed a weapon, something to fight his way back to the vehicle. Joe slid a metal trashcan from across the room and placed it in front of the door. It would at least provide warning if someone, or something, tried to sneak in behind him. Joe moved along the wall of the store and saw nothing but empty shelves. A sign hanging from the ceiling near the back read backpacks/camping gear. Joe moved in the direction, his hopes crushed when he saw them picked clean. He knelt down, pondering his situation, eyes searching the floor.

"You've got to be kidding me."

At the bottom of the shelf was a small pink-and-black "Hello Kitty" book bag. Joe shook his head disgustedly then reached down and lifted the bag. He opened the compartments and dumped the bag's tissue paper stuffing. Joe continued to the back of the store through camping equipment to find an open tent with no poles, empty sleeping bag boxes, a cast iron skillet, and a large coffee can filled with tent stakes. Growing frustrated, he moved on into the game areas. A bin filled with basketballs and footballs and an empty rack where baseball bats would have rested — everything was gone.

Joe walked with his head down, searching; on a bottom shelf was a box of pool balls and a carbon fiber pool cue, stronger and less brittle than wood. Having no other weapon, he reached down and lifted the cue. It was a little long so he unscrewed and separated the thin upper section. Now the weight of the bottom half felt better in his grip. He slapped it into his open palm and felt the sting… it needed more. He looked down at the box of balls then peeled open the cardboard and removed the triangle before searching until he separated the eight ball from the rest. He held the black ball against the length of the stick and smiled.

In his youth, at summer camp, he had learned to braid and weave rope. In one class, he learned to lash stones to the ends of sticks to make tomahawks. Looking at the perfectly shaped shaft and round ball, he had a better idea; if he could locate enough rope, he could weave this into a mace. On his way to the back office, he had his only bit of luck and spotted a wall of climbing gear. Once again, all the axes were gone but there was plenty of coiled nylon rope.

Grabbing a bundle of rope, Joe pushed on the office door and entered the back room. Small and damp, light shone in from a large hole in the ceiling to show everything in the back office tossed over and ransacked. Joe smiled when he looked at the back wall; at shoulder height, rested a first-aid kit with the latch closed. He moved toward it quickly and placed his hand on the cover, closing his eyes and taking a deep breath before he opened it. The kit was untouched and full of goods. He dumped the contents into the Hello Kitty backpack.

Relieved, his mission for medication now accomplished, he relaxed the tension in his body and checked his wind-up wristwatch—still plenty of daylight. Joe cleared a spot on the floor then dropped down to begin building his mace. He weaved the rope, heating it with his Zippo to make it adhere tightly to the form of the cue, strengthening it while he wrapped it around the handle, and firmly attaching the ball to the end. As he weaved, he imagined the damage it would do. With the top firmly attached, he felt the weapon's weight and swung it, feeling the power. Later, he would have to find some varnish or heavy resin to lock it all into place, but for now, it would do. Joe-Mac stood before taking a short swing and crushing a coffee pot resting on a small desk then smiled.

"Yeah… This'll do."

Chapter 5

The long and tall HEMTT bounced and rolled with every pothole. Brad's teeth vibrated as he choked on the diesel fumes that wafted in over the sides of the long cargo bed. The lieutenant allowed them to tag along on the patrol, but having no extra room in the security vehicles, stuck them in the M977 with the work party. Brad scanned the faces of the young soldiers, male and female alike, armed with rifles, wearing Kevlar helmets and body armor. Brad and Brooks dressed in camouflage combat shirts and stripped-down Kevlar helmets. With most gear becoming scarce, they were resupplied with the essentials. At the center of the truck bed, there was a long pile of shovels, axes, and rakes. The soldiers' faces revealed fear and worry, but mostly exhaustion.

A USMC LAV-25 scouted the way out front and an Army Bradley took up the rear position. As the convoy drew closer to the fire, they picked up traces of the pungent smoke mixing in with the diesel. Brooks tapped him on the arm and pointed to the west at the thick column of black rolling smoke.

He pointed down at the shovels in the center of the truck. "They ain't fighting that with shovels."

"Then why are we here?" Brad asked.

The truck's brakes crunched and the passengers all shifted forward then jerked as the vehicle made an abrupt stop. They heard the sounds of the squeaking tracks as the Bradley drew closer then scraped across the pavement, turning so that it blocked the rear deck. Instead of dropping a cargo gate, men hoisted a specially crafted ladder over the edge and attached a side to the truck's bed. Brad and Brooks moved to the front of the line, getting out of the truck before the chain gang started unloading their equipment.

Brad went down first, dropping to the ground and stepping away from the truck. Soldiers and Marines in full kit were already spreading out and forming a perimeter. He watched a pair of soldiers uncoil a long strand of barbed wire. Brooks dropped to the ground behind him, and then turned toward the front of the convoy. The clack of a suppressed rifle caused them to crouch down. One of the security members looked back at them. "Don't sweat it; just the snipers up front."

Brad shook his head at the soldier's comment and continued. The LAV at the front was parked perpendicular to the HEMTT, its turret aiming into a far-off town. Two scout snipers were lying prone across the top of the armored hull. The lieutenant was standing near the rear ramp of the LAV. Young and wiry, his uniform pressed, he was clean-shaven and wore a shiny pistol on his belt. He held a partially folded map in his left hand, comparing it to a list of coordinates on a sheet of paper.

Brad strolled up next to him and said, "If you're looking for the fire it's over there."

"I know where the fire is at; what I don't know is where all the Primals are," he snapped. "Morning air recon had that town covered with them. Where did they all go?" He folded the map and stuffed it into a cargo pocket then looked to the front of the LAV, where a group of soldiers had clustered. "Sergeant Johnson, get a recon patrol ready."

Brooks stepped forward, looked at the map, and then made a 360. "Fire may have pushed them out of the town and into the woods… maybe across the road here. That smoke is still a hell of a long ways off though."

The lieutenant looked up, nodding his head. "That's what I'm afraid of. They get across this road and into the woods, the only thing on the other side is Savannah's perimeter; the packs shouldn't be this far ahead of the fire."

Brad looked back at the lieutenant. "What's all this got to do with fighting a fire?"

"Fighting a fire? Ha! No, the colonel sent us out here to establish an observation post. He wanted us to pinpoint and track Primal movement ahead of the fire, try to turn them if we can."

A young sergeant cut to the rear of the vehicle with four other men close behind. "Sir, we're ready—"

Brooks lifted a hand, catching the young officer's attention. "Lieutenant, why don't you let me and my partner here join your patrol? They might need help if this horde shows up."

The lieutenant looked away, staring into the forest on the east side of the road, then back toward the far-off town. "Okay, but you're just along for the extra firepower. My man's in charge."

"No problem, sir. And could I make a suggestion?" Brooks added.

The lieutenant sighed and looked Brooks in the eye. "I'm listening, but make it quick."

Brooks moved closer and spoke low so that the patrol standing behind him could not hear. "I say to hell with this post you're setting up, sir… get your men mounted back up in the trucks, weapons out and ready to fight. Have the LAV ready to come get us if shit goes sideways. If you have any pull, I'd request to get that Predator back in the air."

The young lieutenant looked Brooks in the eye again, and then casually swept the surrounding terrain. "Thank you for the suggestion. I'm sure we can take care of ourselves." The lieutenant backed away and looked at his squad leader. "Patrol to the village center then report back to me for orders."

The young sergeant nodded his head then looked to Brooks and Brad. "Roger that... Petty Officer, Sergeant Turner, we're moving; if you want to tag along, now's the time."

Brad nodded and turned back to face Brooks, who shot him a grin and stepped off following the patrol leader. Brad pulled his rifle into his chest and fell in line with the rest of the men as he moved ahead of the Bradley and through a break in the concertina wire. As the men moved out, he spun back and saw that the lieutenant had not heeded their suggestion; he was still posting his men around the perimeter and forming a small observation post.

Brad's mind flashed back to a time, months earlier in the deserts of Afghanistan, to a patrol on the other side of the planet. Moving on, patrolling ahead while the remains of his unit formed a similar ill-fated perimeter. His foot fell hard against the pavement as tension twisted the muscles in his back.

"No, this isn't Afghanistan," he whispered to himself.

A soldier near Brad turned to look back. "You say something, Sergeant?"

Brad swept his head left and right. They were moving in a staggered column down a two-lane blacktop road—high grass on the left and right sides, tall trees fifty feet off the road to the right, and open field to the left. They were less than a few football fields from the first buildings straight ahead. Brad was walking two paces behind Brooks, who moved quickly to stay next to the patrol leader.

Brad looked up at the soldier to his front-left. "Nahh, just thinking… you patrolled this road before?" he asked.

"A few times, but mostly by vehicle—just route recons. We usually stick to the city side of the fort; that's where most of the action's at."

"So what's the story back here?" Brad said.

The soldier slowed his pace and looked back over his shoulder. "Back here?" He put his right hand up and pointed far down the road. "Ain't nothing back here or anywhere else. It's all rot nowadays. I don't even know why we waste our time on these damn patrols. This town up ahead… been through it a half dozen times; nothing but Primals in there."

Brad picked up his pace so that he could fall in next to the soldier. "How many?"

"Not a lot; we cleared most of 'em out, but they filter down from the northwest. Guess that's why the colonel wants us to keep an eye on the place. In case the fire pushes more at us."

A soldier walking point far ahead of the patrol put a fist in the air. The rest of the men slowed their advance and spread out, taking a knee around a central portion of the road. Brad passed through the circle and knelt next to Brooks. They stayed together while the sergeant in charge of the patrol jogged forward to speak with the point man. They were nearing the mouth of the small town. Looking left and right, Brad noticed how exposed they were on the open road. He could feel the electricity in the air as the hair on his neck began to stiffen.

"We need to get off this road," Brad said.

Brooks' head stayed in motion, searching the distant structures and tree line. "You see something?"

A gunshot cracked.

Chapter 6

Dust swirled thick, moving across the neighboring city in a dense cloud, blocking out the sun and pushing a cold breeze ahead of it. Turner stood at the edge of the warehouse roof, watching the sandstorm building strength. It twisted as it moved from street to street, blocking his view of the rooftops in the distance, the tan buildings quickly concealed by the snarling sand.

Turner pulled down his goggles in anticipation of the storm and spit dust onto the roof. "Looks like it's going to be a good one, Cole," he said.

A young soldier stood beside him, watching the sandstorm through binoculars. He lifted a hand, pointing to a distant intersection. "Don't seem to bother the Primals much. Look at the dumb bastards; they don't even run for cover."

Turner chuckled as he looked in the direction Cole pointed. A small pack of Primals moved along a street, the wind battering their clothing, knocking them left and right as they moved into the thick mass, probably drawn out by the sounds of the storm. Turner watched the massive cloud grow; they would need to take shelter if it did not change direction. He looked down at the satellite phone resting on a small bench. The signal strength was still spotty, fading in and out. That was the only reason he was up on the roof to begin with. It had been nearly twenty-four hours since it was recovered from the capsule. They kept it powered on and used the vehicles to charge it; still, with the fading signal, Turner was skeptical it would ring at all.

He took the phone in his hand and looked at the display. Even on the roof, with a clear view of the sky, he was having trouble getting two small bars and now the battery was down to twenty percent. "Might be time to call it a day and button up for this storm," he said. "Hard enough to stay clean without these damn sandstorms pushing grit into every crack on my body."

Cole looked away from the binoculars. "We got some time; they might call, and we don't want to miss it."

Turner picked up the phone and turned it in his hand, considering powering it off and storing it. Suddenly the phone began to buzz. Turner looked up at Cole, flashing his tobacco-stained teeth. The receiver showed an encrypted number on the display. Turner carefully held it in his hand and pushed the green "answer" button before holding the phone to his ear. Turner had spent the last twenty-four hours rehearsing what he would say; he memorized a series of questions that he would ask. This was, after all, their first contact with the outside world since it all went to hell.

Now, with the phone to his ear, Turner's mind drew blank and he stuttered, "H-hello?"

"This is Lieutenant Colonel James Cloud of the Coordinated National Response Team. What is the status of your party?" a formal voice responded.

"Wha—huh?" Turner mumbled.

"Are you in command?" Cloud asked.

"Uhh… yeah—yes… yes, sir."

"And what is your status?" Cloud asked, his voice softening.

"We're alive, I guess; I don't understand what you are asking."

"Who am I speaking with?" Cloud said.

"Oh right—this is Sergeant First Class Turner, Echo Company, Second Brigade, well, what's left of it."

"And how many are with you, Sergeant Turner?"

"Ahh… there's ten of us—soldiers, I mean, but I also got lots of local nationals under our care."

"Listen up, Sergeant Turner; I don't have a lot of time before we lose the signal. We are en route and will be arriving south of your position in less than twenty-four hours. We will be landing on the Hairatan road on the south approach to the city; satellite and drone surveillance shows a clear stretch large enough for our aircraft. Do you understand?"

"Wait… you're coming for us?"

"Sergeant, at twelve hundred hours tomorrow, your men must be standing by; we can only remain on the ground for a short time. Refueling has to be spot on for this to work and we only have so much fuel; we have to stay on schedule. If you are not ready to board after we roll to a stop, we will not be able to stay on the ground and wait for you. Have your men ready; pack only yourselves, your personal weapons systems, and one three-day bag."

"But, sir, I got more people here—"

"I will have seats open and a weight allowance for twenty-five personnel—you figure it out, Sergeant. Twelve hundred hours, tomorrow, do you understand?"

"Uhh, yes, sir," Turner said.

"Good, activate this phone again when you are on location south of the city. Cloud out." The phone clicked dead.

Turner lowered the phone from his ear then used his thumb to press the button, ending the call. Cole pushed in close to him excitedly.

"Well, what did he say?" Cole asked.

"I think we're going home," Turner said, a smile slowly spreading across his face.

Chapter 7

"You know you can stay here, Shane; there's plenty of room," Chelsea said. She watched as Shane knelt down to Ella's level, kissing her forehead. His usual ritual before returning to his own quarters.

He turned and looked up toward Chelsea, catching her concerned look. He sighed, taking a long pause and using the time to sweep his eyes over the small housing unit. It was a quaint space with an open floor plan, wood floors, and white painted walls. From his position, Shane could see through the small house into the kitchen, where he was just able to catch a glimpse of the back door.

Chelsea and Ella were assigned to one of the many vacant houses located inside the safety of the camp's perimeter. Ella was willingly placed in Chelsea's care. Shane had his own place just down the street. Because of his injuries, he wasn't given a job assignment on the camp, and technically being a civilian, was kept out of the barracks and instead placed into a private housing unit far away from the enlisted soldiers. "No, it's okay; they gave me a nice spot. I like it there, it's close and quiet," he said. "And besides, I don't think your friend would appreciate me staying here." Shane stood and turned to the door, gripping the handle. He stopped at the sound of her voice.

"What? Why would you even say that?" Chelsea asked. "Don't even try using him as an excuse."

Shane shrugged his shoulders and looked away. "Just saying it wouldn't be appropriate, is all."

"You can't hide your worry, Shane. It's okay—just stay with us," she said. "We would both feel safer with you in the house."

Ella reached out and grabbed his free hand. "Stay, Shane."

He looked down at the girl and smiled. As he began to speak, the sounds of automatic weapons fire erupted from far away. He easily recognized the sounds. Shane's muscles flexed and he turned back to the door, opening it and stepping out into the front yard, using his body to prevent Ella and Chelsea from following him outside.

To the west, high in the clouds, he could see plumes of smoke. Shane knew a fire was burning west of the camp. More gunfire focused his attention—heavy weapons, fifty caliber, and the distinctive report of a 30mm cannon. He felt the door push up behind him as Chelsea forced her way into the yard.

"Primals?" she asked.

He shook his head. "Not sure; those are heavy weapons... fifty cal, and the other sounds like the main gun on a Bradley. If it's Primals, there must be a lot of them," Shane said, his voice changing to all business.

"Think the fire brought them in?" Chelsea asked.

"No, it's from too far out... way beyond the walls."

The sound of motors buzzing moved Shane's attention to the main road in front of the small house. Vehicles turned a corner and raced by just in front of them. As they passed, Shane could see the trucks were filled with armed soldiers. More gunfire filled the air, followed quickly by the sounds of the camp's artillery battery.

Shane swiveled his head and focused his eyes on the dark clouds of smoke, his ears focusing on the distant sounds of combat. "Something bad is happening out there," Shane said.

"Maybe we should find Brad; he'll know," Chelsea said.

Shane's hand dropped to his hip; he felt the standard-issue Berretta M9 pistol. He took a step further into the yard, the tension in his body rising as the artillery fire increased.

"No," he said. "I want you to stay put for now." Shane turned back, looking at Chelsea seriously. "Get your rifle, and keep Ella inside. You're right — I'll stay here tonight. I just need to grab some things."

"What is it, Shane? What do you think it is?" she asked.

He turned, headed toward his house, and yelled over his shoulder, "Just stay inside!"

Shane ran to the street, slowing to avoid another column of fast-moving trucks. He hit the sidewalk on the far side and moved briskly, wanting to run, but not wanting to aggravate his healing injuries. He turned onto a sidewalk that led to the old officers' quarters—a small stack of what would more closely resemble college dorms or an old-style motor lodge. Shane's unit was located on the end of a row of five units. As Shane passed the fourth door, it swung open and a young soldier in full uniform with captain's bars on his hat rushed out. The soldier shut his door and, after nearly colliding with Shane, lost his balance and tumbled forward.

Shane reached out his arm, helping to steady the man. "Sir, do you know what's going on?"

The officer took a pack he was carrying in his left arm and shouldered it as he spoke. "There is a unit in contact a couple miles out. They are in trouble, calling in everything we got to support them."

"Primals?" Shane asked.

The captain shook his head and stepped back. "No, it's contact with an enemy force. They got ambushed on the road—some of the other patrols are taking fire too. Sorry, I gotta go."

Shane watched the officer run down the sidewalk in the direction the soldier-laden trucks had traveled. Enemy contact? Shane said to himself. Why… who would attack an Army base?

He moved back to his apartment's door and entered the space. Shane's room was small and arranged like a hotel suite: a small bed on a long wall, a bathroom at the end, a small kitchenette in a corner, and the opposite wall filled with a dresser and wardrobe.

Shane always kept his bag packed; he found it at the end of the bed and lifted it with his right arm, feeling the scar tissue protest under the weight. He pushed an arm through a single strap then opened a top drawer on the dresser and removed his M4 rifle. He then took several full magazines, which he dropped into the cargo pockets on his pants before he grabbed the last magazine, loaded, and charged his weapon. With his gear, he turned and left the room, moving back to the sidewalk.

More men loaded with gear were leaving the units and running in the direction of the trucks; Shane, growing more concerned, picked up the pace back to Chelsea's house. More gunfire erupted, this time closer, near the gates—small arms and explosions, possibly grenades. Shane began jogging across the street; he saw movement in a far tree line and paused. Silhouettes cut through the thin trees, the fading sun creating deep outlines of their forms. Not the hasty or primitive movement of Primals, but something else. He identified two distinct figures. Shane ran forward and pressed against the corner of a neighboring home one away from Chelsea's house. He peered around the edge of the home, still listening to the truck traffic moving behind him and the steady echo of small arms fire.

Shane focused on the figures and watched them step along, stalking their way through the trees. He saw more file in just behind the first two. "Maybe a roving patrol," he whispered. Shane quickly sprinted to the next building; he passed the door, hoping Ella and Chelsea were locked in as he'd asked. Shane dropped on his belly, low crawled to the corner, and peeked through the tall grass.

Who are they? Shane thought as he watched the man at the front of the column approach the edge of the field that formed the backyards of the homes. The man stepped a few feet into the tall grass and dropped to a knee. Shane saw the man raise a fist, halting the rest of the patrol, then lift a small rifle to his eye—presumably using the optics to scout ahead. Shane's heart skipped a beat when he recognized the black uniform.

It can't be… not here. His stomach filled with fear.

The sound of vehicle wheels screeched as it skidded to a stop behind him, and Shane turned to see a Humvee; a soldier stood in the turret looking directly at him. The front door of the Humvee opened and a soldier stepped out, pointing a flat hand.

"Hey buddy! What the hell you think you're doing?" the driver yelled.

Shane opened his mouth to speak, to tell them about the men in black, but not before a suppressed round hit the standing soldier square in the chest. The driver looked back at Shane with surprise on his face. Shane looked back at the trees in time to see a second muzzle flash. The Humvee's turret gunner came alive, firing high, his rounds ripping up a trail of dirt. Shane turned back and saw that the machine gunner was hit but still trying to operate his gun.

The turret gun went silent as the gunner succumbed to his wounds. The men in black seemed to have not noticed Shane; they must have been attracted to the Humvee's sudden stop.

Probably thought the soldier's yells were directed at them. Shane backed away from the corner, still on his belly. He slowly rose to his knees as the house front door swung open. Chelsea rushed out, carrying her rifle and pulling Ella along close behind. Shane stood quickly and grabbed her arm.

"Shane, there are men back there! Same as be—"

He held a hand to his lips, silencing her.

"Quickly, follow me," he whispered.

Chapter 8

The aircraft banked hard, creaking as it turned. Cloud felt his stomach drop and his ears pop; he looked to the left and could see the tan of the desert and gray of the mountains through his small portside window. The drab gray passenger compartment sat empty, rows of seats ran down the center, and more webbed jump seats lined the outer walls of the fuselage. Cloud looked up, stretching his neck and staring at the exposed ceiling filled with twisting conduits and mechanical tubing.

It wasn't his first time on a military transport. Back before he received orders to ride a desk, Cloud had done his share of rotations to the sandbox both as a battalion and company commander. The desk life was easier on the family but harder on his ego. The field kept him young, the desk made him feel old. He looked around the plane and shook his head. In those days, this aircraft would have been packed shoulder to shoulder with men armed to the teeth and bulked up with armor and equipment. A real can of whoop-ass they joked, crammed into seats so tight it was hard to breathe. Cloud looked down at his feet and closed his eyes; he knew those days would never come back.

His headset squelched to life. Cloud shifted his focus and looked to the front; an airman waved to catch his attention and spoke into a microphone. "Sir, we are thirty mikes out, on approach."

Cloud pressed a switch on the cord of his headset; he acknowledged the call and unbuckled his lap belt before walking to the front of the aircraft. An enlisted man in a baggy green flight suit stood near a bulkhead; he approached Cloud when he saw him then handed off a yellow headset connected to a long coiled cord. Cloud took it in his hand as the man leaned in close and shouted over the drone of the engines, "Sir, the satellite phone is all linked up, ready to dial on your order."

Cloud nodded and put on the headset. He pulled on a wire frame and set the microphone just in front of his lips. Cloud closed his eyes and took a deep breath before signaling the airman with exaggerated thumbs up, the indication for him to place the call. Cloud heard a series of clicks as the call bounced through satellite relays, searching for a viable connection. It took far longer than usual but Cloud knew the network was degraded; some of the analysts even predicted the entire system could be down in less than thirty days.

With no one left to steer and align the birds, the orbits would degrade and eventually they would fall to the ground. A loud, steady tone and the simulated dialing noise focused him. Cloud rehearsed his lines in his head and waited for the call to connect. A solid click and static buzz filled his headset.

"Sergeant Turner here," a metallic voice said.

"Sergeant, we will be landing soon; are you in position?" Cloud said.

Turning his back, Cloud moved away from the airman to make his way across the center of the aircraft. Finding the cabin wall, he placed his arm against it for balance then leaned forward to a window where he could see the fast-moving terrain below. He felt the pilot starting the plane's descent.

"Ah… yes, sir. We are on the north end of the Hairatan road, just past where the roadway opens up."

"Understood. We are on approach; the aircraft will land in your direction, and we will spin one eighty and drop the ramp. Do not approach the aircraft until the flight crew directs you onboard. Do you understand?"

"Yes, sir. But, sir, I have a—"

Cloud interrupted, speaking over the man. "As long as you understand; any other questions can wait. See you on the ground, Sergeant." Cloud removed the headset and made a slashing movement with his hand. The airman disconnected the call and quickly crossed the aisle to retrieve the yellow headphones.

"Sir, you will want to strap in; we'll be landing soon," the man said.

Cloud looked at him apprehensively; he let his eyes drift over the rows of seats to the open cargo bay of the aircraft. Along the back wall near the ramp sat a group of eight men dressed in all black, armed with submachine guns and M4s, pulling on hockey helmets, and dropping tinted goggles over their eyes. Not military men; government contractors originally brought on for a paycheck, now working for whatever it was the general promised them. It was no secret that the contractors had the best food, best housing, and most freedom of movement within the facility. It caused envy among the military technicians living within the walls of the bunker, but that usually went quiet when it was time for them to go out on a mission.

"Are they ready?" Cloud asked, looking back at the recovery team.

The airman nodded his head. "Yes; as soon as the pilot gives the all clear, I'll drop the ramp and they'll make the recovery."

The overhead cabin lights went from green to red.

The airman looked at Cloud. "Sir, you really need to get strapped in."

Cloud shook his head and moved to the cabin wall, dropping into a webbed jump seat. He was eager to be on the ground, to recover the Hairatan group, and make the exchange. The sooner he could get the general's mind off the girl, the sooner he could focus on getting support for his family. So far, any attempt or effort he made to discuss their recovery was thwarted. Cloud was beginning to think that his family was nothing more than a pawn to the general, a carrot dangled in front of him to keep him under control. Everyone had a weakness and the general knew his.

Many of the men at the facility had already deserted, returning home or fleeing to one of the safe zones. After the initial facility lockdown and safely withdrawing from the meat grinder, all available resources were moved into re-gaining control of the nation. Region by region, they used everything they had to help secure bits of the country and to pick up allies within what they then called the secure zones.

Eventually, most of the country was segmented into local alliances and locked in safely behind walls. They formed a new means of communication between them and took control of their local military assets. That left the Coordinated National Response Team obsolete, and even unwanted. As national resources were depleted and more and more requests for assistance had to be denied, the CNRT fell out of favor.

The CNRT was slowly blocked from accessing military bases and airfields, their freedom of movement greatly restricted. State governors demanded the CNRT disbanded and its military might and fuel reserves transferred to local government control. The general stood a hard line, arguing a need for a central government. His words were ignored, but all of that changed with the discovery of Aziz and a race for a cure. Now the CNRT was back on mission, and the alliances knew it. Some were once again cooperating with the CNRT, while others — like the Midwest Alliance — were hunting their own vaccine.

The general knew that finding and controlling a vaccine would be the last chance at pulling the nation back together; control of the cure would unify the alliances back under the CNRT.

The plane bucked hard and rattled. Cloud heard the wheels dropping and the whine of the gear lowering into position. He looked ahead and could see the airman calmly sitting in a rear-facing seat, waiting patiently. The plane bumped hard against the road, and then he heard the wheels squawk as the pilot applied the brakes and the engines were reversed. Cloud felt his body move forward with the deceleration of the plane. The aircraft came to an abrupt halt and then spun around.

The airman jumped to his feet and ran to the back. Light filled the fuselage as the ramp dropped. Cloud unbuckled his lap belt and got to his feet. He moved to the rear of the plane just as the last of the men in black filed down the ramp. Cloud walked to the last row of modular seats and stood waiting with his hands on his hips. The ramp was down and obscured in bright dust; he couldn't see beyond the bottom of the platform.

"Sir, we have a problem," the airman called out. "Could you please join us on the ramp?"

"With the aircraft?" Cloud asked.

"No, sir; the count… Please, sir, I think it would be easier if you came down here."

Cloud grunted; his right hand reached up to check the Glock in his shoulder holster as he said to himself, What now?

He moved through the open cargo space and to the top of the ramp. Standing next to the airman, wearing multi-cam trousers and a brown cotton shirt, a bulky, bearded man materialized. Beyond the pair, he could see the recovery team formed up and surrounding a ragtag band of civilians and soldiers alike, all standing in a cluster clutching children and bundles of belongings. Soldiers were in a guard position, watching the road. Cloud took them out of his view and marched directly to the airman and the bulky man.

The bulky man's rifle slung behind his back with the barrel pointed down just visible near his hip. No rank on his uniform, the man's posture identified him as a senior non-commissioned officer. When the pair saw Cloud, they moved in his direction; approaching swiftly, they met him near the bottom of the ramp. Although the dust still swirled from the aircraft's engines, the bulky man attempted to force his way ahead. Cloud stepped forward and began to point a flat hand at the stranger when the airman positioned himself between them.

Cloud ignored the airman and looked over his shoulder at the newcomer. "Sergeant Turner?"

The man shifted to the right to make himself seen. "Yes, sir. We're all here; what's the hold up?"

Cloud looked at him sternly. "Sergeant, how many are in your party?"

Turner hesitated, then looked up and locked eyes with Cloud. "One hundred and twenty-six—including women and children, sir."

"Do you think this is a game? I told you twenty-five!" Cloud shouted.

Turner took half a step up the ramp; his eyes swept the rows of empty seats, he turned and looked into the expansive empty cargo bay, and then he looked back at Cloud. "Sir, I can't leave anyone behind. If we take our guns out of the fight, these civilians are good as dead. Even with us here, I don't think anyone will survive the winter."

"That's not our problem, Sergeant. I'm ordering you to get your men on this plane."

Turner shook his head. "Not going to happen, sir; you can court martial me," he put his wrists together, reaching to Cloud. "Do what you want, but we won't leave these people behind."

Cloud turned and walked back into the body of the aircraft, fully prepared to kick Turner off the plane and order the pilot to take off. His thoughts flashed to his wife and daughter—the real reason why he was here. "Dammit," he shouted. Cloud spun on his heels and looked the airman in the eye, "Get them on board!" he said.

"All of 'em, sir?" the airman asked.

"Yes," Cloud answered. "And Turner? You can count on that court martial."

Turner smiled and moved to run out of the aircraft to recover his people. "Yes, sir," he called over his shoulder.

Chapter 9

Darkness quickly filled the valley as the sun dropped below the distant mountains. Joe sat huddled in the sporting goods store armed with his newly assembled battle mace. His left arm was swaddled in strips of torn canvas that he had wrapped and tied tightly to serve as protective armor. Joe's back was pressed against the counter, his eyes level with the bottom sill of the storefront's window.

Figures paced along the street, moving slowly toward the grocery store parking lot. Joe's eyes traveled along the dark lot to the row of trees where he'd left his truck. Two hundred yards — a couple football fields — is all he'd need to cross. If he ran, he could be there in minutes. The creatures still followed predictable patterns; they would continue to be drawn to the store for at least the next day and then slowly they would dissipate, returning to the smaller hunting packs. Joe didn't want to wait that long; he was hungry and thirsty, and he wanted to get back to the cabin.

He sat silently watching another pack pass by his current position then readied himself in the doorway. He made sure the things were out of immediate earshot then readied his hand on the door. Letting his right hand firmly grip his handmade weapon, he squeezed tightly, feeling the sweat on his palm. His heart rate increased, adrenalin beginning to surge in his body. Joe checked his pocket a last time and felt the straps of the tiny backpack to ensure it was tight to his body.

"Well, guess it's time to do this," he whispered.

Joe-Mac let the door glide open and stepped into the dark. He stood on the sidewalk in front of the store. The immediate area was empty, but he could hear the plodding of the creatures' feet as they slapped pavement far ahead. He turned away from them and walked down the street, putting distance on the pack. Instead of moving straight for his truck in a diagonal line, he decided he would navigate the long way down the street and cut back up to it, hoping to stay hidden in the shadows of the storefronts.

The moon drifted out of the clouds, its lunar light making the concrete appear blue. Looking into the lot, the figures lit by the light looked ten feet tall and made of steel with their backs turned to him as they moved away and filed into the market. Joe passed in front of a brick-faced auto parts store at the end of the block and paused, crouching low. He heard the sounds of crunching glass. His body tightened, his head moved left and right, but he was unable to pinpoint its source.

Joe heard a loud gasping and intake of air; he spun on his heels and saw a female staggering toward him. Dressed in rags, her left leg moved awkwardly; the clothing at the knee ripped away to reveal torn muscle. She lunged forward, the sounds beginning to gurgle from her drooling mouth. Joe knew she was going to make the howling noise, the one that alerted the others to prey. Not hesitating, he launched himself at her, pushing off with his toes like a sprinter in the blocks as his arm swung up violently. The rope-encased eight ball connected solidly with the woman's temple, her head snapping up and back from the force of the mace. Joe heard her neck crack as her body lifted off the ground, following its head.

She thumped to the pavement and lay still; her head turned away and showcased a concave dent where the mace had struck. He planted his feet and recovered, crouching and waiting for the next attack to come. His head swiveled and his body turned while searching; he picked up the sound of running feet, soon followed by the distant moans. Joe turned toward the truck and ran. He could see the dark line in the distance that he knew was the row of trees where his truck was hidden, and he focused on it. From the right, Joe heard a scream; he turned in time to see a man's rage-filled face emerge from the dark. No time to plant his feet, he pivoted while still running forward and smacked the man with a backhanded tennis stroke, catching him in the throat. The man continued to scream as its body went limp and crashed to the ground. Joe leapt away from its outstretched limbs.

More came; he used his canvas-wrapped arm to push a creature away before spinning on his heels and crashing the mace onto the top of its skull. Not stopping, he continued moving ahead until he was at the trees. He ran through them, twisting around foliage as he heard the things behind crash through low-hanging branches and limbs. The sound of the hunt increased as those in the market learnt of the new prey. Finally, he saw the glint of moonlight off the fender of his truck. He made a last-ditch dash, running with everything he had left. Misjudging the distance as his vision clouded from the surge of adrenalin and darkness, he nearly collided with the truck. He grasped the handle and pulled the door open before diving across the bench seat. He quickly twisted and closed the door shut behind him, his palm slapping the lock, securing it.

He heard the mob crash into the truck, pulling back when they made contact, quickly surrounding it. Joe's 1979 K15 Sierra was far from standard. Dan made fun of him, told him he should grab a new one from a lot in the city, or even one of the military vehicles at the roadblocks on the highway. Joe laughed it off and said he enjoyed the throaty sounds of the big V8, but really, he liked the way the old truck looked and the heavy steel it was made of.

The exterior was wrapped in tensioned barbed wire he'd carefully removed from a farmer's fence. So much epoxy and imbedded chicken wire coated the rear window, it was nearly impossible to see through. The original side windows and windshield were cut out and replaced with Plexiglas that Joe had painstakingly cut from a bank's sliding front door. He bolted the shatterproof and nearly unbreakable acrylic to the truck's body then used even more epoxy to secure rebar and strands of barbed wire over it before he finished it with heavy coats of mirrored window tint.

The Sierra pickup was nowhere near an armored car, but it had saved his ass from the psychos more than once. Joe reached under the bench seat and removed a red canvas bag. He pulled out a foil package of hard candies and a bottle of water. He drank thirstily while listening to the mob outside pound away at the sides of the truck. They screamed as they leapt into the bed, feeling the planted shards of broken glass and roofing nails pierce their feet. Joe grinned knowingly; he had an argument with Dan about the glass. Joe said the things were reacting to pain. Dan didn't believe him and called the booby traps a waste of time.

In the early days, the things would run through plate glass and raging fire to get at a survivor, ignoring harm to their own bodies. In the months that followed, they began to regain tactile sense; although not yet to the degree a human would—or even that of a wild dog—more like a… well, Joe didn't know what to make of them. Regardless, they were changing and that worried Joe the most. Like the female; did she really bump into Joe by chance, or did the others push her ahead and use her as a probe in the shadows to find him?

The truck began to shake violently as the mass surrounding it intensified. Joe exhaled loudly and stuffed a piece of the hard candy into his mouth; he crushed it with his teeth then chased it with another long gulp of water. He sat up in the driver's seat. The moon cast thriving shadows all around the vehicle's hood. Through the heavy tinted glass, it was hard to make out individual shapes. The noise of the mass was deafening; they beat and pounded on the hood of the truck, snarling when their skin or hands would find the barbed wire.

Joe grinned. He liked this new life—although filled with fear, hardships, death, and starvation, he felt it suited him better than schoolwork and juggling odd jobs. Even before all this, life could have been easier in the city, but he loved the mountains and his big trucks. Joe would rather spend a day on a roof than trapped on an assembly line or in college; he figured that could all wait for later. He was working as a ranch hand for Dan when it all started. The job didn't pay much, but it kept him fed and gave him a place to stay.

Dan was strong and capable. Retired Army—or maybe a Marine, Joe couldn't be sure because Dan never talked about it. He was a hard boss to work for, but he kept Joe honest. He saved Joe's life several times at the start of things, teaching him how to move around and how to conceal the property to keep people out. Although, nobody ever came except for some of Dan's family and a neighbor from farther up the mountain. Joe frowned when he thought of Dan. He was really going to be pissed about him losing the gun.

Joe grinned. "Well, I better get back before the old man throws out my stuff and gives away my bed."

Joe let his hand search the steering column; he gave the keys a quick jingle for good luck and turned the ignition while he pumped the gas pedal. The truck roared to life; he revved the engine in competition with the mob's roars. He felt the engine's vibration combine with the pulsing and rattle of the mob. Even though he should be afraid, the mass made Joe-Mac smile. His hand searched the ceiling, finding the switches to the light bars. He flipped all of them on at once, and bright halogen lights illuminated the space in all directions.

They pressed on all sides against the truck, howling, pushing, and shoving to get closer. The protective wire was gashing and slicing away skin; some ignored the pain or were just forced into the jagged glass from others pressing it forward. Joe searched the crowd, looking for the one. There was always at least one. The one that kept its distance, the one that would push a wounded female out ahead, or organize a mob. Joe dropped the truck into four-wheel drive and let it ease forward, the V8 having no trouble moving the crazed out of its way.

He drove slowly, allowing them to follow alongside. He spotted the loner at the end of the tree line; she stood alone. Broad shouldered, long matted hair, nearly naked to the waist, she looked directly into the bright lights of the truck, not flinching. She didn't run at him like the others did. She didn't howl. She seemed to study Joe in the same way he studied her. Joe kept the truck moving in a slow, straight line; then when he was less than fifty feet out, he pushed the pedal to the floor. The truck accelerated hard, throwing the creatures off the hood, bouncing them to the sides. At the last moment, he cut the wheel sharply and aimed for the broad-shouldered woman. She looked at the truck then her mouth opened wide as her body tensed just before the impact. The steel brush guard crushed her frame, the momentum tossing her up and over the cab of the truck like a rag doll. For a moment, Joe thought he saw a look of recognition on the woman's face, that she knew what was about to happen… that she knew she was about to die. In that moment, she almost looked human. He gripped the wheel tight and pushed the ideas from his mind.

Joe steered out of the sharp turn, looking for the center of the road. Maintaining his speed, he cut the wheel hard and the tires squealed as he drove onto the tiny main street. He left town, driving fast. He needed to get distance on this group before he hit the narrow mountain trail that would take him back to Dan Cloud's cabin. The old man would for sure shoot him if he brought back any stragglers.

Chapter 10

Rounds snapped overhead as Brad pressed his face against the grass, his left arm clawing at the ground. His fist balled up to grip the roots of the thick crabgrass, using all of his strength to drag himself forward and off the road while earth spit up from the ground as bullets smacked close by. With his body now in the grass, Brad pulled his rifle to his chest and rolled until he thudded up against a rotting log. He pivoted to his elbows and pushed his head up over the log, bringing his rifle in front of him.

Ahead, he could see that the point man and sergeant in charge were both down, their crumpled bodies not moving. More rounds pecked off the road, spitting dust and shards of concrete with them. Brad saw soldiers lying motionless to his left. Just feet away, a young soldier lay with blood pooling from a wound in his head. Looking into the town's row of buildings, he saw the glimmer of a muzzle flash and puffs of blue smoke. He raised his rifle and tried to focus on the faraway windows.

"Get some fire on that building!" Brooks shouted. "Get your weapons up!"

Brad pulled the trigger, firing rapidly and hoping to suppress the far off gunner. A M249 Squad Automatic Weapon opened up somewhere to Brad's right. The tracers arced through the air, painting swaths of smoke and splinters across the wood-sided structure just below where Brad saw the flash. More fire erupted from the far side of the road as the patrol rallied and brought their weapons on line. Someone fired an M203, the woomp of the weapon followed by the blast of the 40mm grenade. The grenadier's fire was true and the building's front flashed in a blast of white smoke; the roofline crumbled, turning the white smoke to black.

At the same time the gunman ahead fell silent, they heard the eruption of fire to the rear. Blinded by the crest of the hill behind him, Brad couldn't see the vehicles they'd left on the other side. The sound of an AT4 anti-tank rocket screeched and echoed with the crack a large explosion. An M2 machine gun thumped as small arms joined the chaos. Black smoke boiled over the hill; he knew the Bradley, and possibly the LAV, took a hit and was dead or disabled by the looks of the oily, rolling smoke.

Brad lifted his head off the target building; the small patrol was in disarray and the three remaining members were showing fear. On the verge of panic, the soldier Brad spoke to earlier screamed, "What do we do?"

Brooks leapt to his feet where he'd been concealed in tall grass; he quickly took charge and ordered the SAW gunner to keep his weapon pointed and covering the front.

"Anything moves, kill it," Brooks said.

Brooks grabbed another man and laid him in position near the gunner. He moved ahead and searched the terrain; his eyes locking on Brad, he pointed and then waved an arm to the hilltop. Brad rushed to his feet and met with Brooks, already at a slow jog moving toward the hill. He pointed and grabbed the third soldier, ordering him to follow. As Brad approached the hilltop, the gunfire decreased and was quickly replaced by the moans of the infected.

Brooks dropped to his belly; the others joining him on the ground, they low crawled forward to the top of the hill. Looking over to the far side, their worst fears were realized. The HEMMET, LAV, and Bradley were engulfed in flames, men lay dead in the wire, and others were running on the road, back in the direction of the base. From the forest, a horde of Primals appeared out of the shadows, screaming as they charged at the disabled vehicles, swarming into the wire and pushing their way through to the down and wounded soldiers not able to flee.

"This ain't right," the soldier muttered. "Who is attacking us?"

Brooks pushed back into the cover of the hill, ignoring the man, and turned to Brad. "Get these guys back—this is a fight we can't win."

"Back to where?" Brad asked.

"Into the town, get them into cover. I'll join you soon; I need to recon ahead and see what's going on here."

Brad looked at him confused. "What else is there to see?"

"Primals didn't fire those rockets and kill those vehicles. I want to see who did this—now find these guys some cover," Brooks said.

Brad attempted to argue, but could see by Brooks' closed expression that the order was not up for discussion. He turned and looked into the scared face of the man to his right. Brad scooted back on all fours, and then rose to his knee. He looked at the soldier. The man stared at the ground absently.

Brad looked at the man's chest; his armor concealed his nametape. "What's your name, soldier?" Brad asked.

He answered without looking up. "Roberts," he said.

"Listen up, Roberts; we're moving back down the hill. I need you to get your shit together, you hear me?"

The soldier raised his head to look Brad in the eye. "Okay, Sergeant; I hear ya."

"Good, we need to move. Let's get the others."

Brad stood, then reached down and pulled the soldier to his feet. He glanced back at Brooks, who was still lying at the top of the hill, hunched over his rifle. Brad shook his head then guided the soldier ahead of him; together they took off for the bottom of the hill to regroup with the others. "Earlier, you said you've been through this town before, right?" Brad asked.

"Yeah, a few times."

"Good; you know a place we can hide in? Something we can defend?"

"I know a place," he answered.

Brad stopped just short of the others and quickly got them on their feet. A short stocky kid with the word Axe written on his helmet carried the squad automatic weapon. The other, a lanky soldier with stubble on his chin cradled an M203, his vest nearly filled with 40mm grenades. Brad began to speak when he heard the loud roar of an infected moan. The sounds grew louder on the far side of the hill.

Brad pointed ahead to the small village. "Let's move; Roberts has point."

"Where we going?" Axe asked. "What about the others?"

Roberts shook his head and stepped off. "They're all dead."

Brad put out a hand and moved the two men out, and then stepped off next to them. "Come on, pick up the pace; we need to get out of the open."

As if someone was listening, a small group of three Primals broke between the buildings; still over a hundred meters ahead, they moved quickly in Brad's direction, although they didn't see the soldiers. Roberts dropped to the prone position—the others followed his movement—then raised his rifle but paused before firing.

"What do we do, Sergeant?" Roberts asked.

Brad knew if they fired, the mob on the other side of the hill would be on them. "Any of you have cans?"

The men shook their heads and looked at him absently.

"Shit, of course not," Brad said. He reached into his hip pouch and retrieved his suppressor then screwed the can to the end of his M4 barrel. He did not have subsonic ammo so he was still going to make some noise.

"You all hold your fire and be ready to run," Brad said.

He raised his rifle up and aimed center mass at the first jogging Primal and waited for another to move in directly behind it. Brad pulled the trigger smoothly and felt the rifle react; the report from the rifle was muffled, although the supersonic round cracked as it moved down range. Brad lost the sight picture; he lifted his eye away from the optics and watched as the lead runner tumbled forward. Then the second runner stumbled and staggered, the round having successfully passed through the first and into the second. Brad scanned left, finding the third Primal that continued up the hill and not seeming to care about the rest of its party. Brad locked onto it and fired again, watching the round impact it just below the collarbone. The second Primal was still stumbling forward; Brad again aimed center mass and pulled the trigger, watching it crumple to the ground.

He scanned left and right, quickly confirming all three on the ground. "Move, move, move. Roberts, get us off this road and into the trees," Brad said.

The others were already running when Brad jumped to his feet and jogged ahead to join them. Roberts led the group off the road and into the tree line, where they continued jogging ahead until they were deep into the cover of the woods. Roberts stopped next to a tree, dropping low and gasping for air; the others fell in beside him.

"What the hell are we doing, Sergeant?" Axe asked.

Brad knelt next to him and took a drink from his canteen. "We just need to find a place to hole up, Axe," Brad said. Loud explosions echoed in the distance, thunderous booms following a cadence of explosions.

"Damn, that's 105 from the camp!" Roberts exclaimed. "What the hell are they shooting artillery at?"

Brad shook his head and put the cap back on his canteen. "I don't know, but we're sure as hell going to make sure we live to find out," Brad said. "Roberts, find me a hideout."

Chapter 11

The sounds of battle intensified, the noise echoing in from all directions. Heavy hanging smoke drifted over the trees and covered the grounds. Shane pushed ahead, keeping the girls close behind him; he needed to create distance on the last contact with the men in black, but also needed to get into cover. He made a straight line back to his small apartment, where they could regroup, gather supplies, and decide what action to take next.

Shane moved to the end of a long block building that sat next to his own, tall neglected bushes lined the foundation of the structure. He needed to rest; the pain from his partially healed gunshot wound was causing him to sweat and lose focus. Shane got close to the building, pressing his right shoulder against overgrown vegetation. He motioned to Ella with his left arm down and let her tuck in behind him while he kept his rifle aimed forward and constantly searched. Chelsea moved up next to him, kneeled, and used her own rifle to cover the rear approach. Shane turned and saw she had a suppressor attached to the end of her rifle.

"Where are we going?" she asked.

Shane kept his eyes on the long apartment building, slowly scanning along the row of lower apartments before checking the upper level. It appeared empty; nobody was moving in the area, even though more gunfire echoed nearby, and he thought he heard the sound of an explosion from Chelsea's house. The sounds of Primal moans carried along in the wind; they sounded close—possibly inside the fences. The combat was surrounding them.

"We need to dig in; I was thinking my place."

"Shane, you're bleeding!" she said pointing.

Shane dropped his hand down to his thigh. When he pulled it away, he saw an oily stain on his tan leather glove from the blood that ran from the chest wound. It wasn't the first time he had broken it open; he must have done it yet again.

"It's fine. I just need to change the bandage. I probably got it to bleeding by crawling around on the ground back there," he said. "Listen, I'm going to run ahead and get the door open. When I signal, bring Ella up."

Chelsea turned her head. "No, we go together; you're hurt."

"Dammit, I said I'm fine," Shane grunted.

Chelsea got to her feet and stepped ahead. "Just hold onto Ella. Stay behind and cover me; I'll call you when it's clear."

Not waiting for a response, she moved in front of him, and Shane watched as she quickly slipped into the smoky mist. He turned and looked at Ella when she grabbed his elbow and squeezed his arm. After taking her into the camp, where there was safety and protection, he hated forcing her to return to the run-and-hide past they had recently escaped. She was just becoming normal again. Under Chelsea's care, she was beginning to play and even laugh on occasion. Shane forced a smile to relax her, and she put her head against his arm as he coerced his legs back into motion. He then rose and felt the blood drain from his head as he stood quickly. Chelsea was correct in taking point; he wasn't back to 100 percent. There was no way he could get them out of this alone.

He could see that Chelsea had reached his apartment door. She dropped down with her back to the wall, looked back at him, and then waved him forward before turning to cover the front. Shane moved Ella to his other side and stepped off in Chelsea's direction. When he saw Chelsea lean back against the wall as her rifle came up, Shane turned hard, forcing Ella into the grass behind him as he brought up his own weapon and looked into the obscured void where Chelsea aimed.

Two figures broke through the smoke. Shane took aim on the second, bringing his thumb to the selector switch of his rifle before hearing Chelsea whistle at him. He looked back at her and saw her waving her hand before she shot him a thumbs up. Shane looked back into the void while the two men came closer, and he recognized the SEAL team chief and the Marine, Villegas. Shane exhaled and helped Ella back to her feet. He rushed forward, joining the men in front of the building. Shane ignored their greetings while he quickly opened the door and rushed Ella inside. The rest followed him in and secured the door behind them.

Chelsea moved in and drew the blinds before turning. "Chief, what's going on?" she asked.

Chief Sean Rogers moved across the room to the corner, dressed head to toe in multicam. He crouched down and lifted the corner of the blinds so that he could see out. The Marine, Joey Villegas, pressed his back against the wall near the door, keeping watch through a tiny window at its top. Joey let his weapon rest at the low ready. Sean, seeing that Joey was in position, let go of the blinds.

"We're under attack, the COP has been hit on all sides, and our patrols outside the wire have been ambushed. I bumped into Joey at the barracks. Brad and Brooks are both missing; we thought they might have come looking for you."

Shane looked away from them and pulled his shirt over his head. He then moved into the back of the room, facing a small countertop and sink where he kept a jug of bathing water. He looked in the mirror; as he suspected, the bandage had pulled away from the wound, the scabs torn and bleeding. He grabbed and peeled away the bandage before using a gauze pad to clean the wound. He looked over his shoulder at Sean. "I saw some guys, the ones in black, same as back in South Carolina."

Sean's chin lifted, not attempting to hide the shock in his voice. "Where?" Sean asked.

"They fired on a vehicle in front of Chelsea's," Shane said. "Caught them sneaking up through the trees behind her place."

"Did they see you?"

Shane clenched his teeth as he used an alcohol swab to wipe around the outsides of the wound then dabbed it with an antibiotic cream. "No, I don't think so, but it sounded like they did more shooting after we left."

Chelsea helped Ella onto the bed that sat in the center of the room. "Do you think they are here for—?"

"Doesn't matter," Sean said. "They hit the walls and blew a big ass hole in both fences. Many Primals got in; the attacks pulled most of the troops to the outer perimeter. Makes sense now... the bad guys are trying to get everything away from her."

Joey kept his eyes on the door's small window. "Explains why it's turned into a ghost town out there."

Shane finished applying a new bandage and put on a clean shirt. "I saw trucks loaded for war headed west; maybe Brad and Brooks went with them. Most of the officers around here were bugging out in a hurry. One of the people I bumped into out front said there were troops in contact outside the wire. I was headed back to get the girls when I spotted that group in the woods. I was planning to get us toward HQ."

Thinking to himself, Sean exhaled loudly, then turned back to the window and peeked out. "It's a solid plan, we need to break out of this void and get ourselves surrounded by friendlies. The COP is liable to cut this area off and clear it later by sector. Depending on how may infected got in, we could be cut off for days in here."

Shane opened a dresser drawer and removed a tactical vest with loaded magazine pouches positioned across the front and sides. He undid the Velcro and slid the vest over his head.

"I see you're adjusting to civilian life," Sean said, looking at the overloaded gear.

Shane shrugged as he pulled two frag grenades from a sock drawer and added them to his kit. "Better safe than sorry, right? Chief, I'm ready to go when you are; I'll carry Ella."

Chief looked at him, frowning. "Nahh, I don't think so. You're looking pretty busted up."

"Now wait a min—" Shane began to protest before suddenly being interrupted by Chelsea.

"It's okay, I've got her. If I get tired, I'll switch off. Can we please just get the hell out of here?" Chelsea said.

Sean crossed the room and stopped near Joey, who still had his eye to the window. "How's it looking?" he asked.

"All clear, but the smoke is getting heavy; if we're going to move, we should make it quick," Joey said.

Chapter 12

"A hundred and twenty-six! What did you do, bring the entire city? You know I can't allow them all into the mountain," General Reynolds said, his voice sounding tiny over the phone.

Cloud sat at the front of the aircraft, looking back into the fuselage. The aircraft was filled with families and soldiers. Scared and weary, faces covered with filth and dust. Mothers holding children — most likely their first time ever on a flight — while Afghan men sat in groups, looking at Cloud suspiciously. He couldn't blame them; even the US soldiers in their party had their reasons not to trust him. Coming out of nowhere to retrieve them after going months with no contact, he would have no excuse if they questioned him on it.

The line cracked and buzzed in his ear, ending his trance. "Sir, I didn't have many options; the men on the ground refused to leave the civilians behind."

"Well, you should have left them."

"Sir?"

"It's not worth arguing about. We no longer need them; find a remote spot. I need you to drop them and R.T.B."

Cloud's jaw clenched and his brow tightened in disbelief. "But, sir… what about the mission… the exchange?"

"Colonel, there's been a breakthrough with Aziz. We've already made other arrangements. The exchange is no longer necessary; now un-ass that excess cargo and return to base."

"But, sir, I have them all on board now… women and children… our soldiers; I can deliver them," Cloud said.

"Colonel, you have your orders; clean up your mess and return to base. I will have a new flight plan sent to the cockpit; we are showing an open airfield on your current route. If the soldiers want to stay on board, that is approved. If not, land and leave them with the rest. I'll brief you on the changes when you get back."

Cloud grew agitated, his blood beginning to boil; why travel all this way, give hope to, and now abandon these people? The general had lost his humanity; after this, there would be no bargaining to recover his family. All the months of Cloud's frustration were coming to the top, blurring his judgment; he was tired and ready to quit. He had done everything he was asked to, but he could not do this. "You just expect me to leave them? Sir, how am I—?"

His voice crackling in the headset, the general shouted, *"I don't care what you have to do. Dammit, James, I'm trying to make this an easy decision for you. If you can't handle it, put me through to the recovery team leader and I'll have him open the ramp and run them out!"*

Cloud reached up and disconnected the call. The airman moved across the aisle and retrieved the headset. "Cut the link; I won't need it any longer," Cloud said.

The airman looked at Cloud suspiciously. "Sir, we will not be able to receive inbound calls," he said.

"Cut the line," Cloud answered. He turned his head and looked to the back of the fuselage. The recovery team was stretched out on pallets and bundles of luggage in the open cargo hold, weapons still strapped to their chests. The Hairatan soldiers and civilians were all disarmed as they boarded the aircraft, their rifles lay neatly piled and strapped to a pallet under the watchful eye of the recovery team. Many of the black-clad contractors were asleep; others sat looking ahead or playing cards. Cloud slowly got to his feet and walked among the packed rows of seats. At the second to last row, he found the man he was looking for.

Cloud reached out and squeezed Sergeant Turner's shoulder. Startled awake, Turner jumped then looked up at Cloud and rubbed his eyes. "Sorry, sir; first time I've been able to sleep without having to watch my back. Guess I went under a bit harder than I'm used to."

"No worries, Sergeant," Cloud said, smiling. He pointed to a soldier sitting next to Turner. "Sorry, I haven't been able to meet the rest of your unit yet."

Turner looked in the seat to his right, and then threw an elbow to wake the man next to him. "Oh, this guy? Yeah, my right hand man; meet Corporal Mendez."

Mendez let out a loud snort, and then looked over at Cloud; he prepared to stand before realizing he was strapped to the seat. Cloud put out a hand to relax Mendez. "At ease, Corporal. Would you two mind following me to the front? We have things to discuss with the flight crew," Cloud said.

The sergeant nodded. "Is this about the court-martial? I meant what I said back there, Colonel; there will be no disagreement from me. We can leave the corporal and the other men out of this."

Cloud frowned, knowing that Turner and these men really had no idea the condition the world was in. To them, they were just returning home. He'd intentionally misled them and kept them in the dark. "Yes, Sergeant, that's what we need to discuss. Could you both follow me, please?" Cloud stepped back away from the seats and allowed both men to join him in the aisle. He casually glanced over his shoulder and saw that one of the recovery men was watching him. Cloud wondered if the recovery team had already been made aware of the change in plans. With the sat line cut, he doubted the recovery men had their own means of communications.

Cloud moved forward with the two soldiers trailing close behind him. The airman stepped out, blocking the colonel's path. "Sir, can I assist you with something?"

Cloud put his hand on the airman's elbow. "Nothing to worry about. I just need to have a word with the pilots; we have a change of plans."

The airman looked back at the two gruff, bearded soldiers then back at Cloud. Cloud's face was stone. He gave the airman a glare that showed he was losing patience. The airman nodded apologetically and turned to lead the men into a narrow space near the lavatory. He waited for them to catch up before he put his hands on the ladder leading up to the flight deck. Cloud moved in directly behind the airman; he allowed him to take a few steps before turning back to look Turner in the face.

"Stick with me if you want to see your people home safely." Cloud turned back to the front, not waiting for a response. He'd already made his decision and would do what he had to. He moved quickly up the stairs. A small platform at the top led directly into the cockpit. Cloud could see both pilots seated at the controls; two more empty seats were located just behind the pilots' seats. To his left was another member of the flight crew. Leaning over an instrument panel, the man seemed uninterested in the visitors to the flight deck. The pilots themselves either didn't notice the men entering behind them or were unconcerned. The airman stood at the top with his back turned to the pilots while he waited for Cloud and the rest to climb to the top. They were soon all crammed into the tight space.

With the airman's back to the pilot and the crewmember to the left, Cloud used the awkward confines to draw his own pistol. He forced the barrel tightly into the airman's abdomen. When the man looked down and saw the blue-steeled barrel, his body went rigid as his eyes went wide. Cloud let his free hand slide up to the airman's left armpit and withdrew an M9 Berretta from the man's shoulder holster. Cloud kept the barrel tight in the man's gut as he took the M9 and handed it over to a shocked Turner.

After Cloud handed off the weapon to the sergeant, he pointed at the crewmember to the left. Turner looked confused. Cloud used the hand that previously held the M9 and grabbed Turner by the shirt collar, pulling him in. "Disarm that man."

Putting full faith in Turner, he spun the airman around and directed him forward into the cockpit. He stood behind him for a moment before looking back. He could see that Mendez was now also armed and holding the third crewmember at gunpoint. Turner moved up beside him. "Now what? You going to tell me what's going on?" Turner asked.

The airman suddenly bolted ahead, trying to give a warning to the pilots. Cloud was ready for the motion and swung hard at the base of the man's neck with the heel of the pistol. The airman went slack as both pilots turned to look back, and Cloud let the body collapse between the seats. He leveled the pistol at the back of the pilot's head while Turner stepped forward and did the same to the co-pilot. Cloud reached for a hook, pulled on a set of headphones, and watched as Turner mirrored his actions.

"What the hell are you doing?" the pilot yelled.

Cloud looked at both men then sat in the seat behind the pilot, keeping his weapon pointed at the pilot's head. "What's our current destination?" Cloud asked.

"Sir, you know damn well our orders have been changed; you know where we're headed," the pilot answered.

Turner's attention moved to the pilot, suddenly gaining clarity over Cloud's bold move. "Changed how?" he asked.

"Go ahead… tell him," Cloud said. "Tell him the plan to dump these people on a remote airstrip—leave them all for dead."

The pilot laughed. "I'm just a fucking bus driver; what do you want from me?"

"That's exactly what you are, and this is *my* bus now," Cloud said. He reached over the pilot's shoulder and dropped a small scrap of paper. "Here—this is your new destination."

The pilot held up the paper and shook his head. "*Savannah?* Colonel, you've lost your damn mind; he's going to kill you for this."

Chapter 13

The clacking of a swift wind rattling and scraping leafless limbs together woke Joe-Mac from his deep sleep. Joe didn't mind being alone out on mountain roads. He slept the best when he was locked away tight in the cab of the truck. Dan's farm was nice, but there were always people coming and going, slamming doors, and stomping feet. His tiny space in the barn was far from luxurious, but in the truck, he had privacy, and the Detroit steel made him feel safe.

He pulled the edge of heavy quilt down from over his head and looked through the trees into the early dawn sky. Joe pushed the button on his dashboard radio; the blue light of the digital display came to life showing the time as 05:57. The folks at the cabin would be waking up about now and switching out the guards; it would be a bad time to drive up on the gates. Another thirty minutes would be perfect.

He stretched and yawned before reaching across and popping open the glove box; a small thermos and wire contraption dropped onto the floor. Joe gathered up the items and searched the surroundings through the cab windows. It was rare for the infected to move this high up the mountain, but he still needed to be careful. When Joe was sure he was alone, he pulled the door release and let it swing open.

The truck sat in an elevated position just above the mountain road, hidden against an old deteriorating blockhouse. The building was rotting and collapsing in on itself. Empty for decades and concealed by tall trees with drooping limbs, the spot had been long forgotten except by the occasional hiker and weary tourist who may have stopped for a break. As Joe exited the truck, he could see signs of travelers — discarded aluminum cans, the occasional candy bar wrapper, and cigarette butts littered the area. Joe lifted a tin can and examined it in his hands before tossing it to the side.

"Ancient travelers once roamed this place," he said in his best History Channel voice. "Now nature reclaims this bit of the mountain." Joe laughed, entertaining himself as he walked around to the rear of his truck. He passed to the back and opened a steel box that ran the length of the truck bed then opened a small compartment door and retrieved a canvas bag.

He stopped and checked his surroundings again, listening to the sounds of swishing grass in an adjacent field. Other than the trees gently swaying in the breeze, there were no signs of movement — animal, human, or something worse. He took a deep breath and moved away from the truck to an old wooden picnic table. He spotted a small brass plate embedded on the tabletop, the surface engraved with a man's name and the dates he lived. Joe used his thumb to wipe dirt off the plate and read the inscription. "Well, Mr. Tucker, would you mind if I sat at your table?" Joe said. "Guess I'll be taking your silence as a no, and I thank you much, sir."

Joe dropped the canvas bag on the tabletop and set up the wire contraption. He dug through the bag, removed a small metallic disc, and set it at the base of the wire frame. He unzipped a small front pouch and retrieved a zip lock bag; inside were small white fuel cubes. Carefully, he placed one on the center of the disc and held a lighter against it until it produced a dull orange flame. Joe separated his thermos and placed the top cup over the fire, then unscrewed the cap and filled the cup with water. From the bag, he pulled two paper pouches of instant coffee that he slowly mixed into the water.

Joe chuckled to himself. "Boy, Dan would be pissed if he saw me using up my fuel tabs on coffee," he said. Joe laughed again while speaking in a poor impersonation of Dan's voice. "They for *emergencies* only, Joe; why you gonna go *wasting* 'em?"

Every vehicle at the camp was equipped with one of the canvas bags; inside every bag were fuel tabs, instant coffee, soup packets, oatmeal, matches, and bottles of water. Some had a bit more, others a bit less. Joe's bag used to be stocked with chocolate bars and even cans of beef stew. Joe managed to eat up most of his emergency bag on an outing a week ago, and Dan refused to replenish it. Joe scowled, thinking about the lecture he'd received. He started on again mocking Dan. "Joe you need to learn—"

A human voice carried in on the wind silenced him.

Joe-Mac held his breath and knelt down. He lifted a handful of sand and quickly used it to smother out the fuel cube. He heard the voices again, clearer now; although he could not make out the words, he could identify them as two males. The voices seemed to be coming from down below on the road. When he heard the sounds of boots kicking at gravel, Joe dropped to his belly and crawled ahead to the edge of the narrow drive he'd driven up the night before. Through the trees, he could see the dirt road down the steep hill. A man wearing woodland camouflage cargo pants stepped into view just before another man walked up next to him.

The men laughed, one lit a cigarette and used it to light another that he passed off to his partner. They were both armed with military-type rifles; Joe watched as one slung the rifle over his shoulder and turned to look behind him. The low rumble of an engine crept up the mountain road. The men stood together and waited as a black cargo van pulled up beside them. They moved around to the far side of the van to the driver's window. Now out of sight, Joe used the moment to move closer down the hill. He gripped a tree trunk tightly and carefully slid over the edge and into the thicker cover. He cautiously lowered himself down the steep ledge and dropped next to a thick tree.

Joe turned and pressed his back against the trunk so that was looking back up in the direction of the blockhouse then turned his head so that his left ear was in the direction of the van. He heard the engine suddenly die and a sliding door open, followed by the clunk of passenger doors as more men entered the road.

"Chuck, why the hell we stopping here?" a man said.

A raspy voice answered, "Gimme a minute, I gotta take a piss."

The man closed in on Joe's position in the trees. Joe heard him step onto the roadside just yards below him on the steep hill. Joe's heart raced, he could feel it beating in his chest so loud that he was sure the man below could hear it. The man groaned as he relieved himself into the dry leaves. He cleared his throat loudly and spit before turning and moving back to the van.

"They ain't shit up here. How much farther we gonna go up this road, Chuck?" a man asked.

Chuck let out a raspy sigh. "Now last night, you all excited talking 'bout how you saw headlights moving up this road. Now you say they ain't nothing up here. So which is it?"

"Come on now, I'm just saying maybe what I saw is gone. Maybe it passed on through is all," the man answered.

"Or just maybe it's up around the bend with a ranch full of fresh women and hot food; now would you want to pass up on an opportunity like that?" Chuck said.

"No, no, Chuck, I guess I wouldn't," the man said, laughing before his voice once again turned serious. "It's just we been walking all night, Chuck. I think we need a break, or maybe I can ride in the van with you for a spell."

Chuck let out a raspy and deep breathy laugh. "Oh, you want a ride in the van, huh? Cause you special, you want a break, do yah?" Joe heard the sound of a pistol's slide retract as a round was being chambered.

"No… Chuck, don't… I'm okay; I's just—" A gunshot cracked and echoed over the trees. The sudden sound caused Joe's foot to flinch. His boot kicked forward and knocked loose bits of earth and gravel that slid down the ledge, picking up other debris with them as they tumbled. The objects crashed into the dry leaves below.

"What the hell was that?" a man said.

Chuck let out a long wheezy laugh. "What? You need a break too?"

"No, dammit; didn't ya hear that?" the man said, his voice getting closer to Joe as he approached the side of the road. "It sounded like it came from up there."

"Huh." Joe heard Chuck step closer with the other man, Chuck's heavy breathing leading the way. "What? Way up there?"

"Yeah, you didn't hear it? How 'bout ya'll?" the man said, speaking louder to the group that was still gathered by the van.

Chuck cleared his throat again and spit more phlegm to the roadside. "My ears is still ringing from this damn gun… when you all gonna find me a quiet one? Know what? Hell with it. I ain't even in the mood anymore—get in the van, we can move back up here later in the day with the trucks. I'm hungry. Needs to get me some bacon in this belly."

"You sure? It sounds like somebody is up there; maybe we should check it out," the man said.

Chuck let out an exaggerated exhale, his voice turning to frustration. "They ain't nothing up there, probably critters is all. Hell, which of us did time in the Corps? You?"

"No, Chuck; like you told us, you the only one here that's served."

"Good, so that's one thing we clear on. Come on; let's get back to the camp."

"What about the body?" the man asked.

"Get his gear, leave the mess."

Joe heard the clanking of gear being removed from the downed man. Gravel crunched and doors slammed shut then the van's engine roared to life, the driver revving it before making a three-point maneuver to turn it back down the mountain trail. Joe-Mac sat silently until the sound of the van completely faded. He listened to the sounds of the woods, and when the birds' chirping returned, Joe pushed away from the tree and climbed back up the hillside.

He needed to get out of there and quick. *The camp is only two miles up the trail, the guards should have heard the shot; they'd be on alert.*

Joe ran to the table and lifted the cup, gulping down the cold liquid before dumping everything into his canvas bag. He hurried to the truck, dropped the bag into its compartment, and closed the lid. He got into the cab and turned the key; feeling it start, he put the truck into gear and eased onto the steep drive that joined back to the mountain trail. At the bottom, he stopped and placed the truck into park.

He reached over, grabbed the homemade mace—now covered with bits of hair and sticky blood—opened the door, and exited the truck. He swept the area quickly then jogged to the abandoned body in the middle of the trail. The man lay face down in a pool of bright crimson blood circling his head. Joe reached over the body and dug through his empty pockets. Whoever they were, they stripped the body clean; there was no clue as to who they were or where they came from.

Joe sat listening and knew he needed to get back to the cabin in a hurry. Dan was really going to be pissed that he led others up the trail. From what Joe witnessed, there was no doubt that these men were hostile. He needed to get back and warn the camp.

Joe ran back to the truck and drove farther up the trail, checking the mirrors to make sure he wasn't being followed. Dan wasn't going to be happy; Joe broke the rules and entered the trail after dark with his lights on, allowing anyone for miles around to track the moving beacon traveling away from Seneca. It was stupid of him, a dumb mistake, or maybe just dumb luck; hopefully Dan would see it as the latter. Joe slowed the truck and cut the wheel. Pulling to the shoulder, he jumped out and hauled a long cut section of brush away from the road to expose a drive. He drove the truck carefully on the drive and got back out, dragging the brush back over the narrow opening.

Joe drove up the driveway slowly, cautiously avoiding obstacles and navigating the deep muddy tire tracks in the narrow lane. At the end was a tall chain link fence. Joe exited the truck and stepped up to it, banging at the gate. "Come on, dammit; open up!" Joe said.

An old man wearing a striped ball cap and denim coveralls appeared from around a plywood and earthen bunker. The blind was set up so that it was concealed from the gate, but allowed whoever was in it to have a wide field of fire. The old man carried a pump shotgun in his right hand and a cob pipe dangled from his lips. "What's yer hurry, kid? Wuzin' that you doin' the shootin' earlier on?" he asked with a heavy Appalachian accent.

Joe grabbed the gate and shook it. "Damn, old man, will you just open up? No, it wasn't me; we got people moving up behind me… no telling when they might be here."

The old man looked at Joe wide-eyed as he fumbled with a ring of keys. "People ya say? What sort of people? You sure? All the ways up on the mountain cut… ain't no reason for nobody to come up huntin' this-a-way," the old man mumbled. "Unless—was'in ya followed, Joe?" the old man asked.

"It doesn't matter; just get the gate open. I need to talk to Dan."

Chapter 14

The roar of the fire made its way down the narrow main street. Brad moved close to the window and looked out, the distant sky glowing orange. Black smoke seemed to fold over on itself as it boiled and rolled on the wind, growing thicker by the moment. Brooks leaned over the windowsill and fired suppressed shots into the street below, knocking down approaching Primals. Distant explosions and firefights echoed like a Fourth of July celebration from the direction of Savannah.

Brooks had met up with Brad and the team in the brick storefront less than an hour earlier. Covered in soot and smoke, Brooks managed to break away from his scouting mission without being followed. He pulled his rifle from the window and dropped the magazine. "That's the last of 'em. But they're gonna keep coming," Brooks said. He moved up beside Brad and followed his gaze to the distant smoke then said, "Wind is the only thing keeping the fire off us—for now, anyway. If the wind direction shifts, we're going to be in some trouble."

Brad nodded and pulled back from the window. He found a dusty chair and dragged it away from the wall before dropping into it. "How far did you follow them?" he asked.

"Not far; too many Primals once I got over the hilltop, hundreds—maybe thousands—of them moving down toward the base. I'm sure they're at the fences by now… probably explains the arty shots we're hearing. I cut through the heavier woods 'til I lost them then turned back and headed for Main Street. There's a shitload of movement out there. Good thing you all are so noisy and leave an easy trail; I would have walked right past this place on a normal day."

Brad shook his head at the offhanded comment and asked, "Did you see who was shooting at us?"

"No, but whoever it is, it's a bold move starting this fire then leading those Primals to the outpost."

"Leading?" Brad asked.

Brooks pushed rounds down into the magazine to top it off then smacked the magazine's spine against the palm of his hand before locking it back into his M4. "You don't think this was by chance, do ya? The fire, these Primals, the ambush… I'm guessing they lit the fire back behind the neighboring cities then drove up ahead and guided their movement right to the outpost."

Brad looked down at his boots. "But why?" he questioned.

"I don't know. Nobody can take down Savannah without destroying it, and if crazies overrun the place, who would want it? This has got to be a diversion for something."

"A diversion for what? What would they—Ella," Brad said.

Brooks pursed his lips; he turned back to the window and raised his rifle, using the scope to look at the distant intersections. "We need to get back most ricky-tick. I have a feeling things are going to go sideways in a hurry."

The machine gunner, Axe, walked into the room, his boots thumping on the hardwood floor. "Sergeant, it seems clear downstairs; can we get out of here?" he said in a booming drawl.

Brad turned back toward the husky soldier. "How are the others?"

"We good, Sergeant, but not too anxious to spend the night in Primal Central. Roberts was saying he knew of a big old dump truck up the street," Axe said. "You think maybe we could drive it back?"

Brad turned to Brooks who shrugged his shoulders. "Beats walking, I suppose... and if we can't go through the Primals, why not go over 'em."

Brad climbed to his feet and reached for his assault pack. "Okay, let's get moving then."

"Alright, Sergeant," said Axe then turned and thumped back down the stairs to the lower level, his boots seeming to stomp on every step. Brooks turned to face Brad with a grin on his face. "See? Noisy as hell."

"I know, I know. So we have a plan then?" Brad asked.

"Uh huh," said Brooks, moving to the doorway. He turned and looked down the stairs, waiting for Brad to catch up. "But let's see what this truck looks like first."

Brad followed Brooks down the stairs and into the storefront at the bottom. The building was long and narrow. With knocked-over clothing racks and garments lying everywhere, it was obvious that it was formerly some sort of consignment store. Roberts was at the store's front display window with a lanky soldier next to him; Lanky was wearing a worn coonskin cap on his head.

"Soldier, what the hell you got on your grape?" Brad asked.

"Just a hat, Sergeant. I lost my patrol cap when we were running back there," Lanky said.

"And that's all you could come up with? No, no, don't even answer that." Brad stepped closer to the tall soldier and saw *Boone* on the man's nametape. "You any relation to Daniel?" Brad said.

"Nah, well... heck, I don't know... maybe," Boone said.

Brooks moved them to the side and looked out into the street. "I don't care who you're related to. Where is this dump truck?"

Roberts put on his pack. "It's an old tri-axel sitting by a big garbage pile, just up the street at the end of this block on the right. It's one of our landmarks when we patrol this area."

Brooks put his hand on the handle to the front door. "Okay, Roberts, you're on me. Brad, take up the rear with Noisy Boy and Stretch. We move fast and quiet; try to keep fingers off the weapons unless we have to. Any questions?"

Axe raised a hand. "I'm guessing Boone is Stretch, but who is Noisy Boy?"

Brooks made a motion of his palm slapping his forehead. He looked at Roberts and received a nod in reply. "I got it," Roberts said.

Brooks held the door open, allowing Roberts to slip out and disappear to the right. Brooks handed the door off to Boone and followed Roberts into the street. Brad reached back, tapped Axe on the shoulder, and motioned him forward. Axe stepped to the door and stumbled ahead, slapping and knocking over a stool.

"Guess we know who Noisy Boy is now," Boone chuckled.

Axe shook his head at the comment and moved out. Brad ordered them ahead, taking the door from Boone and following close behind. Roberts and Brooks were already at the end of the block. The smoke was growing thicker and obscuring their vision. The roadway was surprisingly clear; abandoned vehicles that had been blocking the streets were pushed to the sides, and wreckage and barriers were removed. Brad turned his attention far ahead and watched as Brooks crouched and looked around the corner. Roberts moved on, crossing the street before turning to wave the others up. Brad walked swiftly, turning every few seconds to check their back trail.

Brooks was still at the corner when Brad reached his position, whereas the others had already crossed the street. Brooks acknowledged Brad then they ran across together to join the rest of the group.

"How much farther?" Brad asked.

Roberts looked back over his shoulder then pointed to an empty lot. "It's right here, around this corner; can't ya smell it?"

The sweet stench of rotting garbage blended heavily with the regular rot of the small town. Brad held Axe back to cover the rear while the rest of the men stacked up on the corner building. Brad moved to the front with Brooks and peeked around to look where Roberts pointed. Beyond the building was a blacktop parking lot entirely covered and piled with garbage. A partially filled dump truck sat backed up to the enormous mound of garbage. Another remnant of the fall, the truck was most likely brought here in an attempt to move the village's waste—obviously, a failed operation—and the now abandoned truck sat as an empty reminder of the town's failure.

As Roberts described, it was a tall, flat-sided dump truck with three large tires under the bucket and a high set cab. The truck looked new, the paint still glossy, the cab doors closed, and windows intact. A white sticker on the door noted the name of a now extinct gravel hauling company.

"Looks to be in good shape; think we can get it rolling?" Brad asked Brooks.

Brooks looked around. "Think the keys are in it?"

Boone pressed ahead and looked at the truck. "I don't need keys, Sergeant; we got trucks and tractors like that on the farm at home. I can get it going."

Brad turned to Boone and smacked him on the coonskin cap. "Well, get after it then. Take Roberts with you to watch your back."

Boone grinned, showing a wide gap in his front teeth, then stepped around the corner and ran to the truck with Roberts close behind. The two soldiers stopped hard when a long burst of machine gun fire ripped from Axe's position. Brad spun around, ready to admonish the SAW gunner when he saw a horde closing from out of the smoke.

"Holy shit!" Brad shouted, raising his own rifle and letting loose a volley of rounds. "Where the hell did they come from?"

Brooks reached down, pulled Axe to his feet by the back of his vest, and yelled "Too many! Get to the truck!"

Axe kept his finger down, walking backwards with Brooks towing him along. Strafing the street, he kept the mob suppressed, knocking down the lead runners while slowing the rest. Brooks made the corner and let go of Axe's vest then dropped in beside him and joined the fight, allowing Axe precious moments to reload. Once clear of the street, Brad stepped out to the right and took up a kneeling firing position, putting rounds down range. He glanced back during a reload and saw that Roberts and Boone were entering the truck's cab; they slammed the door shut behind them and opened the side window. Roberts leaned his rifle out and prepared to open fire.

"Got you covered! Go, go, go!" Roberts shouted.

Brad slapped Brooks on the shoulder to let him know he was peeling off, and then sprinted for the truck. At the rear gate, he jumped and caught the back steel grating of the dump truck's swinging gate. He climbed, and digging with his feet, pulled himself to the top. Spilling over the edge, he scrambled back to his feet and looked over the side. The mass was building and widening at the street's face; Brad could see them swarming from the soldiers' blind spots.

Brad raised his rifle and aimed at the corner position, laying down deadly fire over the heads of Axe and Brooks. Brooks looked back to see Brad on line then moved back again, taking Axe with him. He turned and shoved Axe ahead, then sprinted. Brad kept the Primals back as his friends ran for the truck. Roberts fired from the cab, creating an effective crossfire. Through his peripheral vision, Brad saw Axe jump for the gate; he caught the edge but could not pull himself up. Brooks grabbed his boot and heaved him up. Axe pulled and scrambled before flipping over the ledge and crashing in the garbage at Brad's feet.

As the horde closed in, Brad threw a grenade at the corner, the blast knocking a hole in the closing mob. He turned and saw Brooks' gloved hands reach for the gate. Brad let his rifle hang from the sling, leapt to the gate, and caught Brooks' hands. Using his legs, he pulled his friend into the truck moments before the mob rebounded and crashed into it. Brad dropped and collapsed back with exhaustion, listening to the roar of the crowd surrounding the truck.

Brad lay back in bags of rotting garbage. "Is everyone okay?" Brad gasped over the screams of the Primals. Axe rolled over and pushed himself to his knees; he franticly wrestled with a large black bag and tossed it out of the truck. "Can they get in here?" he asked.

Brooks eased himself up and looked over the gate. He glanced back at the others. "If they could, they already would be."

The truck vibrated and coughed before black smoke belched from the large stacks behind the cab. The truck's gears ground and squelched then shuddered as the truck lurched back. Brad climbed over the bags of garbage to the front. The large dump truck's bucket blocked his view into the cab. He moved to the front corner of the bucket, climbed to the top, and yelled over the edge, "Just drive and get us the hell out of here."

Roberts must have heard his shout; the truck crept back, bumping around as it crushed bodies under the big wheels. Again, gears ground as the oversized vehicle changed direction, and then lurched forward. Roberts guided the truck onto Main Street and headed in the direction of Savannah. Once in the center of the road, the truck's speed increased, creating separation on the pack following.

The speed helped move the stink of the garbage away from the men. Brad looked around the pile and saw Axe at the tail end of the truck, his T-Shirt pulled up over his face and his head hanging out the back.

"You might want to pull your head back into the bucket. We still don't know if there are any more shooters out there," Brooks warned.

Axe put his hand to his mouth and eased back before clumsily falling over and rolling into bags of garbage. He flailed violently, grabbed the bags in his arms, and threw them out of the bucket. Brooks and Brad both burst into unsympathetic laughter watching the big man struggle.

Brad reached out and pulled Axe's flailing body back to a seated position. "Calm down there, hero; save it for the Primals."

Axe brushed a blackened banana peel off his sleeve then put his head back. "I'm sorry—I just have a weak stomach, is all."

Brooks reached into his breast pocket and removed a small, Chap Stick-looking tube. He stretched out his arm to Axe. Axe shot him a sideways glance. "Ughh… no thanks; my lips are fine, and I'm not into sharing lipstick."

"It's menthol… for under your nose, dumbass. Rub it on your upper lip; it'll help with the stench."

Axe took the tube apprehensively and wiped it over his lip as suggested. He took in a deep breath through his nose then coughed, clenching his eyes shut. Brooks snatched the tube back from Axe. "What the hell is wrong with you, man? How's a goofy bastard such as yourself survive the apocalypse?"

Axe shook it off. "That ain't nice, bro," he said. "I got lucky, I guess… luckier than most."

"You been with this bunch long?" Brad asked.

Axe leaned up against the tailgate, being more careful to keep his head concealed behind the steel. "What… you mean Roberts and Boone? Nah, I only been with this group for a little over a week. I worked in supply, but there's a bunch of us on the base these days, and civilians been taking up that work lately. I asked to be moved out here."

Brooks laughed. "Well, that was stupid."

"Yeah, tell me about it," Axe said. "Don't matter—I wasn't any good at that logistics shit, anyhow."

The truck suddenly stopped with a jolt, the engine still running.

"Why'd we stop?" Axe asked.

Brad grabbed the top of the bucket and rose to his feet; they were at the ambush site. The LAV at the front of the column was still burning, its back hatch open with an exposed body lying at the entrance. Behind it sat the destroyed HEMMET with its cab windows shattered by gunfire and its tires boiling in orange flame. The M2 Bradley parked to the rear had also suffered the same fate. The wire still wrapped around the perimeter showed Brad where the Primals had broken through; men in uniform lay dead inside its perimeter. With nowhere to go, the gunfire would have kept them pushed back and unable to fight the Primals, the anti-tank rockets destroying their only protection.

"You think they're all dead?" Axe whispered, moving up from behind.

Brooks spoke up. "Some got out; I saw them move away on foot. Whoever did this probably wanted them to lead the Primals back to Savannah. Nobody here had a chance; this was a deliberate and well-planned ambush. Those vehicles were killed with multiple AT4s. There were a couple machine guns there… and there," Brooks pointed at the tree lines, "to keep heads down while the Primals moved in."

Axe looked at Brooks. "How do you know all of that?"

"Outside of hearing it, I saw the disposed AT tubes and piles of brass. The guys who did this were well equipped." Brooks pointed a finger back in the direction of the small town, at a large group of Primals following them. "We might want to stay ahead of that."

Brad reached over the bed and slapped at its side. "Keep going," he shouted.

Chapter 15

Already soaked in sweat, Shane watched the sky grow dark with the fading of the sun. He hated the night but knew its shadows would protect them, conceal their movement, and make it easier to hide. With the dark, the flashes of light became more prevalent. The tracer fire, muzzle flashes, and exploding mortars painted a picture as it cast shadows through the sparse woods they'd entered while the concussions of explosions echoed and bounced off the heavy cloud cover. They were surrounded; fighting raged on all sides. Smoke, mixed with fog, slowed their movements to a crawl; the Primals or men in black could be meters away and they wouldn`t know it.

The team patrolled ahead through the ever-thickening smoke toward the sounds of the heaviest fighting, hoping to reach friendly lines or an Army patrol. Ella began coughing uncontrollably; Chelsea pulled her to the side and sat her near a low, broken stone wall. Sean saw them and raised a fist then lowered his palm, pushing them to a resting stop. The group bunched up, taking shelter behind the wall. Sean opened a water bottle and took a short drink before passing it back to the others. Chelsea sat next to Ella, rubbing her back, the young girl wheezing from the thick smoke and holding her sleeve over her face. Shane could see she was hurting; even though it wasn't her way to complain, he could see the pain in the little girl's tear-filled eyes.

Joey Villegas came to their side and removed his uniform top then ripped the bottom off his brown T-shirt. He used his share of the water to dampen the bit of cloth before tying it over Ella's face. "There you go, niñita; now you look like a real outlaw. This will help you breathe strong," he whispered.

Shane put a hand on Joey's shoulder. "Thank you; I owe you a new shirt."

The Marine rifleman tried to force a smile but failed. "No worries. If we don't get through this shit, you can have the rest of this one," he said, pulling his uniform top back on. Joey moved away and knelt near Sean. "Chief, we can't stay here. This smoke is fucking with my eyes too; I can't see shit. We need to find a place to hide or get back to friendlies."

Sean leaned out, peeking beyond the wall, then pulled back and sat against the barrier, looking at the group. "The fighting is getting heavier toward main base."

A volley of rounds snapped in the woods behind them. The sound of moans and men's screams joined the fray. Shane tensed up, feeling anxious to be traveling again. The noise seemed to be closing in on them. He checked his rifle to take his thoughts off the dangers and to steel his mind. Shane moved closer and pressed against the wall near Ella. She was curled against Chelsea now, her eyes closed but not asleep. She sensed his stare and opened her eyes to look back at him. Shane removed his glove and put a hand on her head. She grabbed his finger and held it before closing her eyes again.

"I got her," Chelsea said, looking at him. Shane nodded as he took back his hand, pulled his glove on again, and turned to look into the darkness.

When Sean and Joey approached then leaned over them, Shane looked up. Sean knelt down, placing his head close to Shane and Chelsea. "Change of plans; we're going to cut west and make a break straight for the perimeter fence."

"What if the walls are down?" Shane asked.

Sean looked away, searching the night. "The perimeter is close, and there are towers and bunkers on the perimeter, but main thing is they are clear of trees; we have to get to someplace that won't burn."

Chelsea helped Ella to her feet and readied her rifle. "I'm with you, Chief. Let's just get out of here."

Ella gasped. Shane watched her eyes grow large, and he turned his head. He spun and saw a group of Primals dressed in rags lurch out of the smoke. Not wanting to fire his rifle and alert more, he pushed off with his feet, swinging the butt of his rifle as he moved. The weapon connected under the jaw of a charging man. Shane felt the man's head give and his momentum carrying him forward. The man struggled underneath him. Shane used his left forearm to pin the Primal to the ground while he rained down elbows to the Primal's face with his right. He struck until the thing stopped moving beneath him.

Shane looked around, expecting to see more attack. Sean was standing over the body of another, a thin band of smoke rising from his MP5. He grabbed at Shane's collar and tugged him to his feet. "Come on; we got to move now!" Sean said.

Shane stumbled to his feet; he could just make out the figure of Chelsea breaking away through the smoke. He turned and jogged ahead to catch up, the sound of Sean's suppressed submachine gun clacking behind him. A bright flash and a gunshot cracked just to the front, followed by another long burst of rifle fire.

"Oh hell, we're in it now," Sean yelled. Shane felt the push from behind as Sean moved him forward. "Pick up the pace, we gotta break contact."

Shane watched Chelsea continue to the left, her rifle up and firing into the smoke with Ella moving beside her with a firm hold on her pocket. He sprinted to their side, grabbed the girl with one hand, and swung her over his left shoulder; he felt her tiny hands grip his neck in a tight hold. Shane let his rifle hang from its sling and drew his pistol. He jogged ahead, firing rounds at anything that moved to his front. Behind him, he could hear Joey's rifle and the crashing of brush; he hoped it was the team following but didn't dare to look back.

He ran ahead fast, dodging branches. Light glowed from the trees to his front in the direction of the perimeter fences and the field that surrounded it. Shane paused and looked behind, flashes of light let him know the group was still there following him. A figure burst from the tree line to his front right. Not bothering to identify it, he raised his pistol and fired two quick shots, knocking it back. Ella flinched and squeezed his neck. Shane strode ahead and leapt over the downed body, moving slower now and trying to focus his eyes in the changing light. He cut through the final rows of brush and suddenly found himself in waist-high grass.

He spotted an empty watchtower ahead and to the left. Shane turned back and saw Chelsea just behind him; he raised his pistol and pointed to the tower. He saw the recognition in Chelsea's face as she passed him and headed off at a slow jog. Screams erupted to the far right. In the distance near the fence, he could barely make out the bobbing shadows of an approaching mob. A long section of fence was gone, the twisted bits of chain link clanking as the frenzied horde moved over it. Shane stuffed his pistol into its holster and drew a frag grenade; he pulled the pin and lobbed it underhanded in a high swooping arc toward the void in the fences. He hollered, "Frag out," then increased the pace, chasing Chelsea to the watchtower.

Within seconds, the grenade exploded. Shane used his hand to cover Ella's head as he sprinted for the tower. He reached the bottom and saw Chelsea already halfway up the tower's ladder. More gunfire to the rear let him know that Sean and Joey were engaging the mob. Shane grabbed a rung and started climbing, struggling with the ladder as he tried to maneuver his arms and body around Ella, who was now trembling against his chest. Feet from the top, he saw Chelsea looking down from the hatch; she stretched her arms out, ready to grab Ella.

"No," he shouted up at her, "put fire on the mob; give them cover!"

Chelsea looked away and disappeared from the tower's hatch. He gripped the rungs tight and took in a deep breath. Shane reached up and gripped the next rung, pulling with his arms as he pushed with his legs. He cleared the hatch and dropped to his side, crawling away from the opening. He peeled Ella from his chest and placed her in a corner. She scrambled into the small space, placed her hands over her head, and huddled in the dark. He heard Chelsea's suppressed rifle as its flashes streamed light through the tower windows.

Shane forced himself up to his knees then to his feet; he stepped onto the tower's catwalk and raised his weapon. Searching the ground, he saw the parting of the tall grass as the Primals broke through the breach in the fence. To the right, he spotted Sean and Joey in the tree line, firing swiftly. Tracers leaving Joey's weapon sent red lasers of light, which disappeared as the rounds tore through the advancing Primals. Seeing that the men in the trees were losing ground, Shane pulled the last grenade from his vest and threw it hard at the break in the fence. The explosion boomed and blew open a hole in the charging crazies.

The men on the ground took advantage of the explosion and raced for the tower. Shane got back on his rifle and fired into the lead runners, trying to create a separation so Sean and Joey could get to the tower. He watched as Chelsea paused to reload; she slapped a magazine home and continued firing. "They aren't going to make it!" she shouted.

Shane looked down and saw that she was right… there were too many; a branch of the mob had broken away and was on a path to intercept Sean. Shane adjusted his fire to the smaller group, his own tracer fire catching Sean's attention. He saw the larger mob close to within ten meters. Shane clenched his teeth, knowing they would not outrun them to the tower's steps. He gripped his rifle and fired desperately, trying to give his friends cover.

A pair broke ahead from the crowd running nearly vertical to Sean and Joey; he saw Joey smack it away with the spike of his tomahawk. Shane looked on helplessly as his friends made their final stand just yards from the ladder. Another Primal assaulted from behind. Sean flung it past him and stomped on the base of its neck. A blinding light and swirling wind forced Shane's eyes closed, and he looked away from the ground. Shielding his eyes with his hands, he saw a small helicopter above him, shining a bright spotlight down. Farther off, being led to the target by the focused light, two Apache attack helicopters cut in low, driving for the kill, guns spitting rounds.

Following the perimeter fence, the smaller helicopter pulled off and continued down the fence while increasing altitude as the lead Apache let loose a salvo of hydra rockets at the breach in the fence and the field on the far side. Just as fast and with a deafening roar, the tail bird swung around and fired danger close, using its 30mm gun to create devastation among the closing horde.

Sean, ignoring the flying earth around him, sprinted to the tower with Joey close behind. The helicopters continued fighting in tandem, chewing up the remaining mob moving from the break in the fence. Chelsea kept her head down but continued to fire and knocking down anything that got close to the men on the ground. Sean vanished from Shane's sight as he moved near the ladder directly below the tower. Shane looked down and observed that the Primals had thinned out. The spotlight again hit the tower as the three helicopters flew around it in a quick orbit before dropping their noses and flying off again following the perimeter.

Chapter 16

"Where the hell have you been?" A solidly built older man wearing a red flannel jacket shouted from up the narrow drive in a booming voice. He was stomping in Joe-Mac's direction; Joe could tell by the man's furrowed brow that he was fired up over something. Carrying a heavy crescent wrench in his right hand, his left hovered over the antique 1911 strapped to his hip in a cowboy holster, the big US letters branded into its leather side. The gate guard stepped out of the way, pushing Joe toward the old man storming down the path. Even in his mid-sixties, Dan Cloud was an intimidating specimen.

"You know I kept you on here to do work for me, not to go out on these little joy rides. Was that you shooting earlier?" he said, admonishing Joe-Mac from a distance. "Wasting more of my damn bullets."

It was not the first time he had been on the old man's bad side. If this job on the mountain were one of his usual gigs, he would have quit it by now over being tired of the abuse. However, when you hire on a week before the end of the world, your future employment options become limited. Shaking nervously, Joe squared up. Trying to push his shoulders forward, he let his arms hang to the side and realized he had grabbed his mace when he left the truck. This time he had important information; Dan would listen to him.

"No sir, it—"

"Don't push your damn peacock chest out at me!" The old man stepped forward and pointed the wrench at Joe. "The damn tractor's broke again; I'm going to need your help to get it—"

"Dan, there are people out there. I saw them on the cut," Joe shouted interrupting.

The old man lowered the wrench and looked at Joe suspiciously. His gray eyebrows raised the way they did when he was trying to solve a problem. "What do you mean there are people on the cut? Nobody travels this way—not this far up the mountain."

The gate guard pushed Joe to the side, looking around Joe-Mac, and shook his head at Dan. "I'm figuring they followed him, Dan."

Dan waved his hands. "Hold up, Gary," he said, throwing his palm up to silence the guard then pointed at Joe-Mac with his empty hand waving him in. "Tell me everything. What did you see, boy?"

Joe dropped his chin nervously, trying to form his words correctly. "Well, I… uhh… I's making coffee up by the old blockhouse—"

Dan walked toward him. "So you're dipping into the damn emergency rations again? Dammit, Joe, the blockhouse is only two miles up the cut! We got coffee up at the damn cabin; you think I prepped all of that shit just to have you go and burning it up every time you get bored?"

Looking up at the trees, Joe bit down on his lip then looked back in Dan's direction with his head down. "You done?"

"Continue," Dan scowled.

"See I's, well, I's up to the old blockhouse making… Well, I was up there 'cause I had some problems in town, and…"

"You get the supplies?" Dan asked.

"I… ah, I got some of 'em," Joe said. "I got 'em in the truck… but, Dan, these folks, I think they are dangerous. One of them killed his own man, and they said they were looking for women."

Dan walked around Joe and stomped some grass away from an old stump then he dropped down, sitting heavily. "Women you say? How many of them were there?"

"Well, I saw two at first. I crawled into the brush to try to get closer when a van drove up. I had to hide so they wouldn't see me. Nevertheless, the man, the one in charge, he talked about having trucks and more men come search the cut. He said they'd come back later."

"Later when?" Dan asked, sitting up on the stump, now fully interested.

"I'm not sure, Dan; the man said they were gonna eat and get some trucks, that's all," Joe replied.

The man looked down at his boots and scratched at his head. "You put the brush back in front of the drive?"

"Yes, sir," Joe said.

"I'm going to send some of the boys out to cut fresh limbs to conceal it. I think you're right though; they'll be back, and they'll find us soon enough. The road shows too many signs of wear for them not to track us to here."

Gary moved forward again. "Probably followed that loud-ass truck the boy's got and the bright lights he likes running on it."

Dan chuckled. "I'm sure they did, but no point arguing about it," he said. "Gary, I need you to stay on watch a couple more hours. I'll send one of the boys down here to back you up." Dan used his empty hand to push himself up to his feet, then spun and turned to look at Joe. "You ain't off the hook; follow me."

Joe stepped off quickly, trying to keep up with Dan as he marched up hill, following the narrow path that headed toward the compound. It was more of a mountain ranch, really… a small cabin with two open barns—one over a hundred years old—the other, a steel building. A rough-cut hobby farm rested in the only bit of cleared land. The cabin was the nicest thing up there; solar and wind powered with a steel roof, it would look right at home in any *Homes and Gardens* magazine.

Talking to Dan's daughter-in-law, Amy, Joe learned it was Dan's wife who had wanted the cabin. It was their dream home—a place to spend their golden years after Dan retired from the Marine Corps. Unfortunately, she passed away before it could be finished. Still, Dan built the house exactly the way his wife had wanted it.

Dan moved up here and spent the next ten years alone. Adding the pole barn later and starting the small farm, he dedicated himself to living off the grid. The old man always had a feeling something bad was coming; he did not know what, but he wanted to be ready when it happened. Signing on to put a new roof on the barn and help harvest the fall crop, Joe was just lucky enough to be doing odd jobs for the old man when it all started.

Joe was also there the day Amy showed up at the cabin with the warning. She brought news from her husband that something happened or was about to. Amy's husband — Dan's son — was some big shot in the Army. He had inside information and a warning to lie low for a spell. Still, they did not know what it was or how long it would last, but Joe figured that as long as he was being paid, he might as well hang out.

Dan had immediately locked the gates and concealed the driveway. He sat by the old C-Band satellite dish day and night, catching news updates and trying to get word from his son. As the world crumbled, he put attention on helping friends and neighbors who lived near the ranch. Soon, the compound was full of people, five families in total. Good people, mountain people, who knew how to live up there. They always had game to eat, and they quickly went to work canning everything they could from Dan's garden.

After things quieted down, Dan let Joe and some of the others make trips into town, but he made them follow a strict set of rules so that they wouldn't be followed back up the cut. Months later, Joe was still here—no longer getting paid, but still alive thanks to Dan. Joe grew tired of Dan's rules and managed to break every one of them, and the more he broke them without paying the price, the more careless he got. He figured everyone left around this area was dead or had moved on. Joe was wrong.

"I see you lost the Sig," Dan said, without looking back. "That stick thing you're holding supposed to replace it?"

Joe bit his lip, not wanting to antagonize the man any more then he already was. "No, sir; I got cornered at the market, lost the pistol and most of my gear. I managed to rig this up at the sports store in town."

"Does it work?"

Joe grinned, looking down at the bloodstains covering the mace. "Good enough, I reckon."

Joe followed Dan to the top of the hill. He moved away from the cabin and proceeded to the steel pole building where a group of four men sat out front preparing for the day's chores. The men carried pistols in holsters, but outside of that, no weapons more useful than a shovel or a coffee cup. They'd never been attacked up the mountain, so there was no need for it. Dan called out to one of the men, ordering him to join Gary down at the gate, and then asked the rest to follow him to the barn. Without hesitating, the men stopped what they were doing and got to their feet.

Joe smiled, watching the way people moved around Dan, not questioning him, just jumping when he asked. Joe liked to consider himself more independent and freethinking than that. Although, he knew if Dan barked, he would be just as obedient—at least while the old man was watching. Joe joined the pack and followed Dan to the old hay barn. He pulled back a large sliding wood door and moved to the center of the floor where bales of hay were stacked.

Dan reached down and hoisted a bale. "Gimme a hand, would ya?" Dan said. The other men quickly joined in, moving bales to the back of the barn.

Joe stood beside them, looking confused. "Ah, Dan, shouldn't we be taking care of that thing I told you about?"

The old man turned and scowled at Joe. He moved back to the center and tossed away the last bale. A trapdoor was located underneath. Twisting the dial, Dan fumbled with a combination lock and then opened the trapdoor. Under the door was a large, dark green, canvas tarp. Dan grabbed a corner and pulled it back, revealing a stack of rifles and cases of food and dry goods.

"Dan! What the hell? Why didn't you tell us about this?" Joe gasped.

Some of the other men began to laugh. "Those that needed to know... know'd," the old man said before dropping into the hold. He reached down, lifted out a large duffle bag, and dropped it to the edge. He unzipped the bag, grabbing for two box magazines, then took a Ruger min-14 from the stack and handed it to one of the men. Quickly, he did the same with another. "You boys take these and head out to the cut; get up high and watch for traffic. Joe tells me that he saw some folks moving this way that might be up to no good."

"Should we stop 'em?" one of the men asked; he was a tall man with a clean-shaven face, wearing a tight gray T-shirt and jeans.

"If what Joe says is true, this crew could be real dirty. Try to avoid 'em. But Kenny, if you see them, get a good count. I need to know numbers — vehicles and equipment. Then get your ass back here, okay?" Dan said.

The men acknowledged the old man and left the barn, leaving just Joe and a straggly kid they called Watson. Joe didn't like Watson; he thought the kid was lazy. The scraggly teen was the type who never left the house before everything happened, more comfortable with a video game controller than a hammer.

Dan moved a rifle to the side and grabbed an old pump-action shotgun. Going back to the canvas bag, he retrieved a box, from which he grabbed a handful of green shells and, one by one, loaded them into the gun. Dan handed the shotgun to Joe, and then passed him the remaining box of shells. "Try not to lose this one," Dan said.

The old man grabbed the edges of the hold and hoisted himself out, then turned and tossed the canvas cover back over its contents.

"Uhh, Dan? What do ya want me to do?" Joe asked.

The old man ignored him and moved off to the side before lifting and closing the hatch. He dropped the lock into position and spun the dial, "Well, Joe, I been thinking on that. What to do with you and the kid."

"Come on now, Dan, you don't want to go grouping me with Watson here," Joe said.

Dan twisted his jaw as if he was chewing a piece of old gum then rolled his eyes back, looking up at the ceiling of the old barn. "Watson, get back to the pole building; get the families ready to move up the mountain," he said.

Watson kicked at rocks while keeping his hands in his pockets. "What you want me to say to them, Dan?" Watson asked.

"Didn't I just tell ya? Get 'em ready to move—one bag each. I'll let 'em know when; now go on." Dan turned and walked to the barn door, moving straight for the cabin then stopped and looked back at Joe. "Come on, let's go."

Joe stepped forward. Using the sling of the shotgun to put it over his shoulder, he wisely kept pace with Dan. When they arrived at the cabin, they found Amy standing on the porch. There was a lot of activity going on at the ranch—far more than usual—and it had obviously attracted the women's attention. Amy was at home on the mountain ranch. Even though she was born and raised in the city, she found that the mountain life suited her. Tall with a tan complexion, she was strong from years of running, trying to keep up with her husband's active military career.

"What's all the commotion, Dad?" she asked.

Dan stopped and looked at her. "It could be nothing, but until I know otherwise, I think you should lead the families up to the other place."

Amy looked at him, surprised, then walked across the porch and leaned against a handrail. "That's close to two days of walking; are you sure?"

"Nah, I ain't sure of much. But even if I am wrong, it don't hurt to get these folks moving around some. And there's provisions up at the lake spot that need rotatin' anyhow. Just get the people up there and settled in. I'll send for you in a week."

Amy stood upright and looked Dan in the eye. "What is it, Dan?"

"Joe says he saw some people on the cut; they might not be friendly. I just need you to do this—get everyone to a safe spot so I can deal with the strangers."

Amy nodded and turned back to the cabin, letting the screen door shut behind her.

Joe stood back, watching and growing frustrated. Dan checked his rifle and began following Amy into the house. "Hey, Dan, don't ya think we should be doing more to get ready?"

The old man kept moving toward the cabin. Entering the covered front porch, he put his hand on the knob and turned to look Joe in the eye. "Son, I've been getting ready for this my entire life."

Chapter 17

The truck bounced through a patch of broken roadway and downed trees. Brad positioned himself high in the bucket to lean over the cab of the truck. Balancing on the piles of garbage as the big vehicle lumbered over potholes, he looked far to the east. The horizon was glowing bright orange from both the flames of the burning fire and the perimeter gate's spotlights. The gunfire had decreased in the last hour; now only the occasional gunshot or burst of automatic weapons fire would break the air.

He lowered his binoculars and moved his attention to the shoulder of the road. Primal silhouettes backlit by orange flames swirled in the tree lines, their hands rising to greet the passing vehicle. Some ran from the burning forest, escaping the flames, and leaving the cover of the trees to pursue them on the road. Some stayed back out of range, following the truck's movements, while others swarmed in close, shadowing to it like parasites. Brad looked at the things near the shoulder and saw worn and ashen faces, their clothing smoldering, hair singed. They held no sign of humanity, like hollowed out mannequins with no soul and no want of anything other than to feed. The thought pushed a shiver through his body.

"This shit is creepy, man. We gotta get out of here," Axe mumbled.

Brad turned and saw that the stocky soldier had moved up beside him, his rifle clutched tightly in his hands. The truck stopped suddenly and Brad fell forward against the cab. He watched as Axe banged into the bucket and nearly tumbled back into the loose bags of garbage before catching himself. Brad used a free arm to steady his body then strained to look ahead.

His attention was caught by the sound of the driver's window rolling down and Roberts shouting, "Sergeant, you need to see this."

Brad gripped the edge of the bucket and looked to the horizon. "Oh hell," he gasped.

"Where do they all come from?" Axe asked.

The truck rested in the center of the empty road. Far in the distance, a deep crowd hundreds of Primals wide and at least a mile long was moving through the smoky mist. They were pouring out of the trees and marching to Combat Outpost Savannah, pushed forward by the fire. Brad felt Brooks' presence beside him just as the SEAL snatched the binoculars from his hands.

"I don't think this was a diversion; whoever did this intended to wipe us out. We're less than a mile from the gate, and that's where the mass is headed."

Axe stepped back; Brad watched the younger man push away from the cab, his hands trembling. "We need to turn around and go back the other way."

Brooks reached into a cargo pocket on his left leg and removed a bottle of water. He twisted off the cap and handed it to Axe. "Here, take it easy, drink this," Brooks said.

"What the hell are you all talking about? Why would anyone want to wipe us out?" Axe sputtered.

"Just drink," Brooks said.

Axe grabbed the bottle and gulped thirstily. When he stopped, he used his sleeves to wipe the water away from his chin, taking in deep breaths before handing the nearly empty bottle back. Brooks took it and put the cap back on then said, "Tell me, Axe, outside of this place, who else does Savannah have contact with?"

"What do you mean? There isn't anything else besides this 'cept a couple holdouts along the coast. Heard there was some kind of thing goin' on in Texas, but nothing like this," Axe said. "We're it."

"Is that the consensus around camp then?" Brooks asked.

"Consen-a-what?" asked Axe, his face screwed up like he was in pain.

"Is that what everyone thinks?" Brad blurted out impatiently.

Axe looked around and nodded. "Yeah— I mean *we are* all that's left. There isn't anything else out there; D.C. is gone, the president's dead. Nothing."

Brooks grinned. "It's not true, Axe; there are people left. Big groups of them from what I have heard, and not everyone is playing nice these days, either. In addition, there is something all of them want, and it's located on Outpost Savannah. Something important."

Axe shot Brooks a confused glance. "What? You mean like food or something?"

Brad let out a short chuckle and shook his head. "There could be a cure, or a way to help us get it."

"Damn! You serious? Then why the hell… I mean, why would someone do all this?" Axe asked.

Brooks reached out and put a hand on Axe's shoulder. "Because they either want it, or they want to keep us from getting it."

"Well…" Axe put his head down then snapped it back up. "We can't let them get it, now can we?"

Brooks shook his head. "No, Axe, we can't."

"How we going to stop 'em? C'mon, there's just five of us, and the whole outpost is being overrun."

"How many rounds you have left on the SAW?" Brooks asked.

Axe shrugged and pulled the weapon in close to his chest. "Bout a box and a half."

"Good!" Brooks reached over the bucket and pounded his fist on the roof of the cab. "Let roll!"

The truck's gears ground and the oversized vehicle lurched forward. Looking to the side, Brad could see that Primals were being attracted to them and gathering on all sides, following them. "Earlier, you said you had a plan. Is this part of it?" Brad asked.

"I lied; I don't have a plan," Brooks responded. "Let's get eyes on the gate and see what's shaking."

Brad clenched his eyes closed tight, trying to block out the smoke. He reached up and pulled his goggles down then grabbed the balaclava around his neck to pull it up over his mouth and nose. The smoke was growing thicker, forming heavy clouds that hung over the roadway. The dying of the sun brought on dark, oily blooms of smoke that glowed with a foul orange as the flames cut through. "This isn't going to end well," Brad whispered, keeping his eyes on the road.

"No, I'm thinking not," Brooks answered.

The truck moved into a tight cluster. Roberts slowed slightly but maintained his course, pushing Primals that refused to move under the large wheels of the dump truck. The vehicle pitched slightly as the bodies crunched under its treads. Some Primals howled and some threw their bodies at the sides of the truck, but most just followed alongside, waiting for their moment. The crowd grew around them, morphing into a tightly packed cluster of burnt and singed bodies.

"There are just so many of them," Axe said.

"Yeah, but it'll make it harder to miss," Brooks said.

The gates of Savannah slowly became visible through the heavy smoke. The sandbag bunkers positioned outside the gate were abandoned. A Humvee sat burning, its entire frame engulfed in flame. Tall chain link fences reinforced with steel plates, tight strands of cable, and razor wire still stood, locked and secured. The mass of Primals pressed tightly against it, their bodies causing the gates to heave and pulse with their movements. Fires raged on the far side of the gates, and sporadic gunfire still rang out from somewhere inside the outpost while the thumping of a helicopter echoed from the south. Two tall watchtowers—one on each side of the gate—were empty, the tower windows shattered.

"Main gate is abandoned," Brad said.

"Guards probably pulled back to defend the airfield," Axe said. "We used to drill that all the time. The perimeter will shrink as areas fall."

The dump truck approached cautiously and stopped in the middle of the road still fifty meters from the gates. Brad pointed to a cluster of Primals on the far side of the fence. "Gates are closed; how did they get in?" he said.

Brooks leaned over the side of the truck's bucket and looked down; Primals in all directions clustered around them, pushing against the truck. Brooks pointed to the right of the gate; a small blacktop road followed the fence. "That maintenance road goes all the way around the camp. Let's follow it. There must be a breach somewhere."

Brad smacked the top of the cab and relayed the instructions. Again, the truck heaved forward as it made its way to the maintenance road that ran parallel to the fence. Navigating slowly, the mass stayed glued to their sides. The truck passed the first of the abandoned bunkers then veered around and down, making a sharp turn between the bunker and the gates then onto the empty road. Brad looked behind and saw the mass shift and roll, heaving and following them onto the maintenance road.

"Wait, stop!" Axe shouted.

Brad slapped the top of the truck, causing Roberts to hit the brakes. He turned, looking at the pale face of Axe. "What?"

Axe looked at them sheepishly. "If we drive to a hole in the fence, we're going to lead all of these things right to it. We'll let all of them in."

Brooks bit his lip, trying to conceal his surprise at Axe's astute statement. He nodded then used his forearm to wipe away the sweat on his brow. "He's right," Brooks said. "We can't stay in this truck."

Brooks jumped out of the bed and onto the cab of the truck; he skidded across its roof then dropped down on the vehicle's hood. His movements frenzied the mob, their screams and moans increasing. Roberts rolled down the driver's window and yelled out, "What the hell are you doing?"

"See if you can get the front of the truck nice and close to the fence."

The truck lurched forward slowly, pushing the Primals out of the way. The front end touched the fence then screeched as it scraped against it. Brooks, kneeling on the hood, showed Roberts the palm of his hand to halt the truck's movement. "Brad, get up here and cover me," Brooks said.

Brad pulled himself out of the bucket and onto the top of the cab; he unslung his rifle and watched the SEAL. Brooks tugged on his gloves, getting them tight; he then slung his rifle to his back. He swiveled his small assault pack around to his chest and readied a section of rope, counting it out and tying a knot at the halfway point of its length. He put his hands to the fence and tugged. "I'm going to climb up and over. If the crazies on the other side notice me, put them down. I'll secure the far side then the rest of you join me."

Axe shook his head. "Hell no, I ain't climbing no fence."

Brooks smiled back at him. "Sounds good; you stay back here and guard the truck. Roberts, get that windshield kicked out; I need you and Stretch over next—Brad, you got me covered?"

Brad placed the stock of his rifle in his shoulder. "I got ya, buddy."

Brooks jumped and grabbed the fence. Digging in with the toes of his boots, he quickly scaled the near side and reached the top bar. He grabbed it with both hands and pulled himself over the top then straddled it and secured the rope. "You got me?" he asked, looking to Brad.

Brad shot him quick thumbs up, and Brooks quickly rappelled down the other side. He dropped to the ground in a crouched stance, readying his rifle and moving out away from the fence. Brooks' position on the ground enraged and attracted the Primals around them. The ones close enough to see pushed against the fence, causing it to sway. "Let's go, Boone; you're next," Brad called out.

The tall soldier pulled himself through the broken windshield. He pulled the rope to check its strength then, as Brooks had, he quickly scaled up and down the other side. Roberts climbed out and did the same. Brad turned to see Axe pacing the bucket.

"Let's go, Axe; waiting on you, buddy," Brad said.

"I ain't good at climbing," Axe answered.

A suppressed gunshot and flash of light took Brad's attention. Brooks was engaging a small group. Three bodies fell to the ground one after another. He looked up at Brad, waving his non-firing arm, urging them to hurry. "Let's go, Axe! No time for this," Brad said.

Axe moved to the front of the bucket and pulled himself onto the cab then crawled across and dropped to the hood. "I'm not sure I—"

More suppressed gunfire from the far side cut him off. Brad saw Brooks firing at a larger group moving from the shadows. He lifted his own weapon and fired at those that were closest.

"Move your ass!" Brad shouted. He kept his rifle on the closing Primals as more broke out of the shadows.

"They're on to us; we gotta beat feet!" Brooks said. "Let's go, Brad; spider man over that damn thing!"

Brad pulled down his rifle and spun it around to his back; he jumped to the hood, listening to the steady cadence of Brooks' rifle. Looking up briefly, he could see Brooks had them under control for the moment. Axe was partway up the fence when Brad tightened the straps on his gloves and grabbed on, pulling himself up with his arms as he pushed with his feet. Scrambling, he was soon alongside Axe. Brad stretched and reached the top bar. Throwing a leg over the top, he locked himself in with his legs then tugging at the rope, he pulled with everything he had to try to help Axe reach the top.

When he was close, Brad lay against the top bar and reached down for the stocky man's harness. He strained and heaved. "Damn, you're heavy," he grunted.

Axe was able to get his right arm on the bar; he pulled up and nearly tumbled over the far side before Brad was able to steady him. Axe was panting, his face covered in sweat. "I told you I wasn't no good at climbing, Sergeant."

"No problem, no more climbing. Slide your ass down that rope; I'll be right behind you."

Axe nodded his head and adjusted his grip on the rope. Grabbing the second section, he dropped his legs over the far side and slid down the rope nearly out of control. Brad heard him thump to the bottom. Not wasting time, Brad grabbed the rope and, gripping tight, dropped over the edge, quickly going hand over hand until his feet touched the damp grass.

Brooks took his eye from the rifle and looked at Brad. "Lead us out; we have to move."

"Where to?" Brad asked, pulling his rifle back to the front. Looking in the direction of the main gate, Brooks raised his rifle and fired more quick shots. The Primals were onto them and more were pouring in from the direction of main camp. To the right was a wide grass field then the trees. Brad saw the other soldiers gathered behind him. Without suppressed weapons, they were unable to join the fight. Brad grabbed Roberts by the collar and directed him to the wood line. Leading the others, the soldier took off jogging and quickly found a trail that led them into the thicker vegetation amongst the trees.

The team crossed into the heavy brush, trading stealth for concealment. The cracking of limbs and leaves was loud, but the heavy ground cover made them nearly impossible to see. Brad stuffed a hand into his hip pocket and removed his compass. He unwound the 550 cord holding it shut and flipped it open. He halted them next to a tree just long enough to get a bearing. No time to retrieve his map, he used the glowing dials to orient himself on the trail; they could move east and hit the main roads of the outpost. Brad unwound the cord and hung the compass around his neck and, using the flat of his hand, he shot a course.

Roberts acknowledged the order with a nod of his head and stepped off, moving carefully now. A branch cracked and Brad spun around, pointing his weapon. His eyes focused on Brooks dropping in behind him. "Wish I would have packed my NODs," Brooks whispered. "Whose idea was it to go exploring again?"

"Yeah, yeah, yeah, day trip, my ass," Brad whispered.

Chapter 18

Light reflected off the ceiling of the watchtower from the flickering of flames, while the sounds of the dry brush and grass crackled as it burned on the scarred earth below. Strands of fence wire and posts mixed with the twisted bodies of the Primals. Flames licked the steel legs of the watchtower, but they were tall enough to protect its occupants from the heat. A light breeze pushed smoke through the tower's windows as the walls rattled with the nearby impact of artillery fire.

Sean took off his rucksack and glanced over at Chelsea, who was pulling a long wooden footlocker away from the wall. He was tired; they had been moving for hours now, and much of it had been fast paced without an opportunity for rest. He sighed and paced away from the window, dropping to the floor in a crouch. "Anything?" Sean asked.

Chelsea used her multi-tool to break the seal off a deep wooden footlocker. She flung the cover open and pulled out three steel ammo boxes. "I got two cans of .223 and one 9mm," she said.

Villegas moved across the watchtower floor and grabbed one of the cans. He broke the steel wire keeping it closed, and then took a stack of cardboard boxes before moving to a corner of the tower to fill his magazines. Chelsea continued to dig through the footlocker, lifting out a case of MREs and a package of water bottles. She used her multi-tool to pop the tie on the case of MREs and removed a tan package from the box. Too dark to read the label, she passed the mystery meal off to Shane. "See if she'll eat something," Chelsea said.

Sean stretched across the floor and reached for the water, removing a bottle from the shrink-wrap. "Smart of them to stock these towers with emergency rations."

Chelsea nodded. Finding the footlocker now empty, she closed the lid and sat on it, pushing her feet away and stretching her tired legs. "How far to the next occupied tower?"

Sean stood and walked to the outer edge of the small space and looked along the perimeter fence. "Half mile, maybe, might as well be a thousand," Sean said. He opened a window, letting in the sounds of battle. "If they didn't abandon it."

Chelsea looked up at him. "One of us should try to get to it; we should send a runner."

Sean shook his head. "No, the birds saw us; they'd have called in our position."

Shane mixed up a drink mix from the MRE and handed it to Ella. She took the bottle from him and drank thirstily; he ripped open a foil packet and smelled the meat mixture. Sticking a spoon into the middle of it, he handed the entire thing off to Ella. She took the packet and returned a sour glance.

"Just try, okay?" Shane said. He turned and looked at Sean. "I saw the contingencies; base security would have closed off the outer perimeters… fell back to the airfield. It's going to take time for them to regroup and get us."

Sean nodded his head. "For now we're safe; we're up high—the steel and block tower legs won't succumb to this fire. We can hold out for a day or two if we ration things out. We stay quiet—the things on the ground will clear out and we can cut through the woods to main gate, or move to the next tower; either way, that fire is going to keep us in place for a while."

"So we just wait?" Chelsea asked.

Sean stepped back and closed the window. "We wait."

"What about those men?" Chelsea asked.

Sean rested his weapon across his knees, dropped the magazine, and inserted a fresh one from his vest. He then leaned the weapon against the wall next to him while he removed more empties from his gear for reloading. "The way I see it, they struck out… came up empty handed. They could sit and search the outpost until our people or the Primals get them. Nevertheless, I would imagine they would go for a hasty extract. They have to know by now that they screwed the pooch."

Villegas chuckled. "I think you're right, Chief; those boys can get chewed on by the Primals here or get their asses chewed by the boss at home. Cause nobody is taking our niñita from us. Right, Ella?" he said, giving the girl a smile.

Ella grinned at hearing her name and took a bite of the MRE. Shane refilled the bottle and handed it back to Ella, content in the knowledge that she was safe.

Chapter 19

Joe ran, trying to keep up with Dan and the other men. Less than thirty minutes prior, the scouts had returned from the cut. They reported seeing three large trucks and at least twenty men moving up the road. The trucks were now stopped at the entrance to the long driveway. Dan jogged down the trail, and then slowed to a walk. He pointed a hand to a tall embankment that overlooked the driveway. The scouts nodded, ran to the position, and dropped into the prone behind it.

Dan continued with Joe trailing close behind him. At the end of the driveway was a tall, steel-tube cattle gate. However, off to far left and concealed in high grass and brush, was an earthen bunker. On an opposite angle to the embankment was where Joe positioned the scouts. The bunker was positioned so that it would flank anyone who approached the gates. If anything happened, the opposing teams would be able to lay a deadly crossfire over the head of the driveway. Like two overlapping funnels, the bunker and embankment held strategic ground over the approach; anyone coming up the driveway would have their eyes on the gate, while men on the flanks took aim.

Joe stayed close to Dan as he made his way to the rear of the bunker. An eight-by-eight structure, it was a small space with a port window cut out and positioned on a natural slope on the grounds. Gary stood inside, looking out the window with the second guard next to him. AR15 rifles had replaced the gate guard's old shotguns, their blued barrels pointing out the small window. Dan leaned and looked into the entrance. "Okay, keep your cool; no shooting unless I say so. But if I give the word, we go at them hard—give them hell."

"I got it, Dan," Gary said, and the second guard nodded nervously in acknowledgment.

An engine rumbled below them on the driveway. A splash of water sounded as a large truck drove through ruts in the muddy approach. Joe looked out, but regardless of the sound, all he could see was green vegetation. The driveway sat buried in a thick, twisted maze of trees. The lane was cut by a bulldozer years ago, when the cabin was first built, with the intention that it would be the only way for vehicles to get up to the ranch. If the strangers wanted up the mountain, it would be by foot or up the driveway.

Dan walked away from the bunker and back to the cattle gate. Joe fell in next to him, holding the pump shotgun anxiously. "Just relax and try to look tough," Dan said. The old man let his arm drop to his hip; he undid the snap on the cowboy holster and adjusted the 1911.

The sound of the truck grew louder as it splashed and thumped up the driveway.

"We should have thrown some logs or something across the driveway, tried to slow them down or stop them," Joe said.

"Nope," Dan reached into his breast pocket and pulled out a cigar; he bit one end off and used a match to light it. "This'll send 'em right where I want 'em. Block the drive and they spread out like roaches."

The front end of a red Dodge Ram broke the cover of the trees. The truck drove just into the clearing, stopping in a sunny spot of driveway. High grass reached up to the running boards of the truck. A second vehicle drove in close and at least one more lagged behind that. Dan stood his ground behind the gate, looking directly into the tinted glass of the Dodge Ram. He took a long pull on the cigar, blew smoke rings, and then turned and spit into the grass. Joe looked at Dan in amazement; with all that was going on, Dan looked bored, as if there were a hundred and one things he'd rather be attending to.

Dan caught Joe's stare. "Poker face, Joe," he whispered.

One by one, the truck engines shut off and after a seemingly long wait, the driver's door opened on the lead vehicle. A bearded biker-looking man stepped out and opened a crew cab door for a shorter, fatter man who followed him. His feet sank into the thick mud, causing him to nearly lose his balance. He let out a string of profanities before grabbing the other man's shoulder and moving onto the higher, more solid edge of the driveway and out of the mud. The passenger doors of the lead vehicle opened and two more men moved out into the driveway.

Aside from the fat man, the strangers were dressed similarly in dark blue shop pants and T-shirts. Fat Man wore corduroy pants and a black leather vest, a stocking cap pulled down low over his brow. All were armed with long guns of the hunting variety and had big knives on their belts. Fat Man had a shoulder holster holding a small black pistol pulled tight over his heaving chest. Upon looking at him, Joe wondered how the man's thigh-sized flabby arms could reach the weapon without help.

The fat man and bearded driver turned away to discuss something before they looked back at Dan. Fat Man pulled a hanky from a pocket, wiping sweat from his brow before raising his hand in a friendly wave. "Hello," Fat Man called out as he stepped away from the vehicle. "It's been a while since we've seen a friendly face." Fat Man continued on, the bearded man walking close by his side. The other two men stopped and took up standing positions by the passenger side of the truck. They left the front door open, thinking they were in cover from the men on the gate. Joe grinned to himself, recalling Dan's assignments, knowing the strange men were now directly lined up with the hidden bunker's guns.

Dan spoke in a low voice as he watched the strangers approach the cattle gate. "Keep your eye on those two by the passenger's side. If shooting starts, I need to know if they went down. You recognize anyone yet?"

"I didn't get a good look, but I know that voice. The fat man waving is the one they called Chuck; he's in charge."

"Hello," Fat Man called out again, still raising his right hand in a greeting.

Dan held his stare and let them get to within ten paces, then spit into the grass. "That's close enough."

Fat Man stopped, Beard pulling up close beside him. Their faces changed from mocking grins to seriousness. Fat Man put his hands in the air, showing Dan his palms. "Whoa now, we don't mean you any harm. This is just a neighborly visit."

Closer now, they could see the bearded man's arms were covered in tattoos, and he wore black leather boots. A bowie knife graced his hip and a large pistol was stuck in the front of his pants. He carried a Savage scoped rifle with notches cut into the wood stock. Fat Man showed only the small pistol, his black vest covered with a random assortment of military patches and a US Marine Corps logo.

Dan let his hand drop and rest on the grip of the 1911, speaking just loudly enough for the two men in front of him to hear. "Is that so? Well, what brings you up my mountain, Chuck?"

The men's faces changed again, this time to shock. The bearded man, for the first time, appeared uneasy. Chuck lowered his hands and put them on his hips; his face flushed and his forehead showed beads of sweat. "You know my name? So you've heard of me?"

"Bits and pieces," Dan said. "So you mind telling me what brings you up here?"

Chuck grinned and let out a wheezy laugh. "You mind letting us in so we can talk? We've got food."

"Oh, it's apparent you've got food, and looks like you've been getting more than your share," Dan said. Joe cracked a smile at the comment and saw that the bearded man struggled to maintain a straight face.

"Listen here, now," said Chuck, his anger building. He paused and took a deep breath. "I'm in charge of things now; all I want to do is get to know the folks still running around here. Take a census, so to speak. Maybe there is something we can do to help each other, things we could trade?"

"Not interested," Dan replied.

"Maybe we have something you need."

"I got everything we need."

"Then maybe you got something we need," Chuck said, the pitch in his voice changing.

Dan took another pull on the cigar. Joe looked out and saw that men from the second vehicle had begun to move forward. He could barely see them at the edge of the driveway but knew there would be more from the third truck doing the same. If they were allowed time to spread out, there would be too many to defend against.

"Listen here," Dan said. "I'm going against my better judgment—but I'm going to make you a onetime offer to turn around and get off my mountain. I want you to forget this place ever existed."

"Or," Chuck asked sarcastically.

Dan smiled, showing Chuck his teeth. He tapped the cigar and let a long ash drop from the end. "Or I shoot you in your guts now, and we can let our men settle this."

Chuck's jaw dropped. "What the hell is wrong with you? I came up here to help you, and you treat me like this?"

Quicker than Joe could think, Dan drew the 1911 and aimed it at Chuck's fat belly. The men near the lead truck took notice of the quick action and stepped forward. Instinctively, Joe brought up the shotgun and rested his sights on the men by the truck. They froze and put their hands up backing away, holding their rifles to the side. "I am about to rescind that offer, Chuck," Dan said.

Speaking for the first time, the bearded man raised his hands. "Come on, now, we'll leave. Come on, boss," the man said grabbing at Chuck's shoulder as he backed away. Chuck staggered back, defiantly being pulled away by the bearded man. They retreated to the side of the truck. The men moved to the open doors and stood discussing something through the open cab of the vehicle.

"What are we doing?" Joe asked.

"Stalling… need to give Amy time to get everyone clear. Get ready," Dan said.

Chuck stepped away from the truck as the others stood near the doors. The truck's door obscured Chuck's right side. Joe looked beyond him and could see the men from the rear vehicles were slipping into the woods on both sides of the driveway. "Dan," Joe whispered.

"I see them, you get a count?" Dan said.

"Twelve, at least, probably more," Joe answered

"Hey!" Chuck shouted from his place by the door. He put up his left hand up and started to walk back toward the cattle gate. Suddenly, he took a long sidestep and his right arm came up holding a MAC-9. Chuck squeezed the trigger; the weapon fired wildly in Chuck's one-handed grip. Dan dove and tackled Joe to the ground. Rounds pinged and sparked off the cattle gate. Gunfire erupted from the guard forces' hidden positions and the Dodge Ram exploded in the crossfire. As Joe rolled away, he saw the two strangers on the left side of the truck crumpled in broken glass. The bearded man lay facedown in the mud. Enemy fire picked up from deep in the woods; a round snapped over Joe's head.

He dared lift it again and saw Chuck waddling into the cover of the trees, running toward the rest of his group. Joe raised his shotgun and fired, racked the gun and fired again. His actions drew more fire to their own positions. Dan grabbed him and led him away, back in the direction of the embankment. Dan dropped into a ditch then rose up, crawling like a professional, keeping his body low as rounds cut over their heads.

They moved out of the ditch just behind the embankment. Joe could hear the rhythmic sounds of the guards' Ruger rifles firing. Through the echo of the incoming fire and the zip and crack of nearby rounds, Dan crawled up behind the embankment. The guards' faces were pressed to their rifles, firing steadily into the woods when he got there. "Keep fire on them. Joe and I are going to sneak around to their flank," Dan said to the guards on top of the berm.

"We're gonna *what*?" Joe gasped.

"Just follow me," Dan answered. Stepping off farther to the right and moving away from the driveway, he used the terrain to stay in cover, keeping high ground between them and the enemy.

Dan slowed his pace, and Joe walked slowly forward, keeping his eyes on Dan's back. They took several steps onto an overgrown path, and then lowered to a crouch. Dan had his pistol in front of him, searching the terrain ahead. Joe caught movement from his peripheral vision as the limbs of a bush moved unnaturally. He turned his head and looked into the eyes of a young man; blue-eyed and blonde-haired, his sneer revealed brown, slimy teeth wrapped in badly chapped lips. Joe exhaled loudly, pointed the barrel, and pulled the trigger.

The shotgun blew a hole in the man's sternum; his eyes went wide as his mouth dropped open searching for air. A second man stepped from behind him and fired a rifle. The round went wide, air zipping as it passed Joe's head. Dan pivoted, raised the 1911 and, firing twice, hit the second man just below the ear and temple. Dan leapt toward the two men and kicked the weapon out of the hands of the first, who still lay gasping for air on the ground, steam leaving the hole in his chest. Joe stood over the man, looking down at his wound in shock. The man's blue eyes twitched and rolled in their sockets.

"Let's go," Dan said, not looking back as he moved along the trail in the direction the men had come.

Joe stepped forward after Dan, and then paused, feeling faint; he dropped to the side of the trail and vomited. He buried his head in his hands, his watering eyes blurring his vision. Dan reached down, grabbed him, and pulled him to his feet. "You'll have time for that later, let's go!"

Joe took in a deep breath and held it then followed Dan close, trying to silence himself and control his breathing. They cut sharply back into the tall ferns. Moving back toward the driveway, Joe could barely make out the metallic skins of the vehicles ahead. He could hear Chuck screaming instructions to his men and the occasional burst of the MAC-9. Dan froze and pointed ahead; just yards away behind a thick oak, a man stood looking toward the embankment. He held a rifle and leaned out, fired a quick shot, then ducked back behind the tree to reload.

Joe lifted his hand to Dan's shoulder; he handed off the shotgun then readied the rope battle mace in his right hand. He walked ahead slowly, lifting and dropping his feet quietly. The man at the tree worked the bolt on his rifle, spun out, fired, and again ducked behind the cover of the tree. Joe was within five feet of the man when suddenly he turned and put his back to the tree. Joe froze and somehow the man did not see him; he was too focused on searching his jacket pocket for more ammo. After pulling out a handful of loose rounds, he struggled to straighten them in his hand when his eyes wandered up and saw Joe, now just feet away, stalking him.

He dropped the rifle and attempted to raise his hands as a whine left his lips. Joe ignored the plea and stepped off hard with his left foot. Swinging swiftly, the mace connected with the man's temple. His legs buckled and he dropped straight to his knees before leaning back to rest his body against the tree. The man's head tilted awkwardly, the neck obviously broken. Dan shuffled forward, leaned over the man, and then used the heel of his boot to kick him flat to the ground. He grabbed the rifle by its stock and tossed it clear of the body. He handed the shotgun back to Joe and led them toward the parked vehicles.

Dan dropped to his belly and crawled toward the parked trucks. Joe fell in beside him, staying low so his body stayed concealed by the tall ferns on the forest floor. They could see movement now—people darting left and right on the other side of the driveway, the guards' crossfire still taking a toll on the strangers. Chuck's screaming continued, his voice becoming more panicked as he lost control. Two men ran from the far side of the driveway and took cover behind the second truck, exposing their backs to Joe and Dan. Dan pointed at them and whispered, "Take the left."

When Dan rose up to his knees, Joe did the same beside him before they leveled their weapons and fired. Dan's round went high, taking his man in the right shoulder. The round then went through and punched a hole in the truck's fender. He fell against it, streaking blood on the truck as he dropped. Joe fired at the second man, the buck shot eating earth from his low miss. The stranger turned; with shock in his eyes, he fired blindly back at them as he ran back toward the third truck.

Dan leaned out and positioned himself, firing into the direction the man fled. Chuck continued to shout panic-stricken orders. Joe heard another volley of the MAC-9. The last truck's engine started and doors slammed shut; Joe started to rise to run after them, but Dan reached out and pulled him back down. "Let 'em go," he said.

"But they'll get away."

The truck backed down the drive, splashing as it went. They heard it crash through the brush at the entrance then gravel crushed as the truck spun its tires, entering the cut. Dan jumped up to his feet and jogged forward. He went directly for the downed man leaning against the second truck. Dan tossed the man's shotgun away then grabbed at his wounded shoulder, pulling him into the open and dumping him on his back.

The man's eyes fluttered. Dan ignored him as he searched his shirt pockets, placing everything on the man's belly. He slapped at his pants, removing anything he found. Joe knelt next to the wounded man and sifted through the pile. An old wallet, pictures of a woman and kids wrapped in plastic, a pack of cigarettes, and loose pile of cough drops. Dan pulled his knife and reached at the man's collar. Joe thought he was going to slit the prisoner's throat when he brought the blade to the man's neck. He tugged at the collar and inserted the razor-sharp blade into the man's shirt then cut downward and split the sleeve, exposing the man's wound.

Dan cut away another wad of the man's shirt, then balled it up and stuffed it into the wound; kicking violently, the man howled and screamed. "Well, hell, you do have some fight left in ya," Dan laughed. He folded the man over, exposing his back. "Help me hold 'em," Dan said.

Joe reached down and clenched the man's neck while pressing his knees against his thighs to still him as best as he could. Dan took another wad of material and stuffed it into the exit wound. Again, the man kicked and flailed. Dan stood and grabbed the man under his good arm. "On your feet, sweetheart," Dan shouted.

The man looked up drunkenly, his face pale and dripping with sweat. He struggled to stand but his legs would not cooperate. Joe grabbed his other side and together they dragged the prisoner back to the cattle gate. Joe prepared to lower the man softly when Dan released him without warning, causing his body to slump and collapse against the ground, his face hitting the gravel. Dan reached down, grabbed the back of the prisoner's shirt, and dragged him against the gate so that he was sitting up.

Dan slapped him on the dirt-covered cheek with his open palm and said, "Wake up."

The man's head tipped back; his eyes parted slightly to look up into Dan's face.

"I stopped the bleeding, but you're still going to die if you don't get some help."

The man stared up at Dan, his eyes squinting. "What do you want from me?"

Chapter 20

Flames burnt bright as the brush crackled in the intense heat. The men sat hunkered down in a dry streambed, huddled together with weapons pointed out. Enraged by the inferno, the Primals ran in chaotic packs, moving in all directions and seeming intent on escaping the heat.

"Out of the pan and into the fire," Brad whispered.

Brooks looked back at him; he put two fingers to his eyes and pointed into the brightest part of the flames straight ahead. "Through there is a pedestrian gate; I remember it from our runs. An open field is on the far side—it's a natural firebreak."

"Yeah, but how do we get through that wall of fire."

"Stick to the trail… it runs right up the middle there. We get through that, jump the gate, and we're in the clear," Brooks explained.

A thunderous crashing of brush turned Brad around. Engulfed in flames, a swarm of crazies burst from the brush. They charged directly at the hunkered-down men. Axe let loose a long stream of automatic weapons fire. Some fell, but the majority of the mob continued on. A large man, his face ashen and black with soot, broke away from the group. Gunfire exploded all around Brad as the man dove and caught him in the chest. Brad was flung back off his feet. He wrapped the Primal in his arms and tried to throw him away, but with his feet off the ground, he lost leverage. He continued to roll, the stench of burnt flesh and singed hair filling his nose as they turned away.

Landing on top, Brad managed to gain the dominate position. The man lunged up, his teeth snapping through burnt and blistered lips. Unable to release the man from his grip, Brad pushed up hard and rained down a heavy closed fist directly to the thing's face. He felt the nose give way, the cartilage crushing under his knuckles. Brad swung down again; striking just below the eye, the crazy's orbital bone took the brunt of it. The Primal paused, the blow momentarily shocking it. Brad used the brief delay to retrieve the hawk from his hip. Leaning back and with a two-handed blow, he landed the spike square into the creature's head.

Brad pulled and retrieved the hawk. Before he could stand, he was yanked forward from behind. Brooks had him by the collar and was dragging him. The other men were in a dead sprint, moving away from them toward the trailhead. Brad swam, struggling to get his feet underneath him. Just as his toes made contact and he lunged forward, Brooks tumbled forward, a female Primal attached to his back. Brad slipped, ducked his head, and dove into a roll. He came up, quickly caught his bearing, and lashed out, catching the female between the shoulder blades.

More were on them; a Primal grabbed at Brad's arm. Unable to ready his rifle because the sling had twisted and wrapped tightly to his body, Brad pulled his sidearm. He stuffed the barrel into the man's abdomen and fired. Looking to his right, he saw Brooks lashing away with his fighting knife, hacking and slashing at the charging creatures. Brad pushed the dead crazy away from him, forced his M4 out and the sling off his arm, and then leveled his rifle. He fired twice, ran to Brooks, and fired another salvo before a stream of tracers ripped past him just to his left, the rounds so close they snapped and zipped by his head. Brad quickly rolled toward Brooks and looked behind him. Axe was kneeling at the trailhead, laying down fire with the SAW.

Brad scrambled forward on all fours. He rose to his feet and grabbed Brooks by the wrist, pulling him up behind him. Together, they sprinted to the trailhead under the cover of Axe's fire; the heat was more extreme out of the dry creek bed. It hit Brad hard, taking away his air, making it hard to breathe. He pulled the balaclava up over his chin and put on his dark glasses, already feeling the flash of the heat against his skin. They jogged down the path until they found a closed gate. Roberts and Boone were on the far side, their rifles leaning over the edge and firing precariously close to Brad, knocking down the pursuing Primal.

The fence was less than six feet tall, but the gate was much shorter. Axe ran directly at it, pushed on the top, vaulting himself over and tumbling to the opposite side. Brad and Brooks followed close behind. They could see the open field now. Just over the size of two football fields, it was covered in thick green grass and patches of open gravel. The fire had avoided it and went around on both sides, leaving the once green grass smoldering at the edges. Brooks grunted and turned the others in its direction. They jogged directly to the center of the field and collapsed to their backs, gasping for air.

Brad pulled at the drinking tube of his CamelBak and took a long gulp, feeling that the bag was almost dry. "How much farther?" he asked, looking up at the smoke-filled sky.

Roberts pushed himself into a seated position, searching the tree lines. "Depends on where they pulled back to. If they collapsed to the airfield, we still got some traveling to do."

"That'd be most likely — huh," Boone grunted and dropped to his belly, taking Roberts with him.

Brooks took notice of Boone's quick actions and rolled to his side. "What is it? What did ya see, Stretch?" he asked.

Boone crawled to the edge of their tiny perimeter, looking out across the long field. "There, near the tree line, do you see them?"

The team pressed their bodies into the tall grass to hide; Brad tried to move and position himself to follow the soldier's line of sight. At the opposite end of the field, the fire burned bright in the trees. Smoke swilled up and rolled into the sky, pushed by the heat of the flames. He searched left and right then froze. Clustered together—much like Brad was with his own group—he spotted a group of five men, dressed in black. They slowly emerged from a break in the burning brush. One was looking to the sky and speaking into a handheld radio. The group walked several meters into the tall grass and dropped down.

Brad turned to look at Brooks, who was already examining them through the optics on his rifle. "Is it the same group?" Brad asked.

"Got to be; why else would they be here?" Brooks said.

The man with the radio dropped his arm and moved across the group. He pressed in to talk to the others then pointed in Brad's direction. They bunched up and stepped off, moving to the center of the field. When they picked up the pace to a slow jog headed straight for them, Brad raised his rifle. "What do we do?" he whispered.

"Wait 'til they get closer; if we have to, we'll take them out."

Still a hundred feet away, the group suddenly stopped. Two turned back to cover their rear while the other two covered the flanks. The man holding the radio dropped back to rest in the center of the group then put the radio back to his ear. The man pulled the radio away and swept the field ahead; he seemed to look right at Brad's team. His hand dropped to his belt and he pulled a smoke canister then tossed it just meters away; the canister popped and bled a thick stream of yellow smoke.

The distinctive whoomp, whoomp of a Blackhawk helicopter faded in; high in the smoke, it still couldn't be seen. "Ahh, shit," Brooks said.

The smoke over their heads began to swirl and the helicopter dropped in on top of them. It hovered overhead then spun, putting its nose into the direction of the wind. Brad looked around; the rest of his men had their faces in the ground, avoiding the smoke and dust being thrown out in all directions.

"Should we fire on them?" Brad yelled over the sound of the helo.

Brooks reached out and pushed Brad's barrel down. "Hell, no! If they don't see us, let them go; the door gunner will chew us up!"

The Blackhawk hovered close then touched down to the ground. Brad used his hand to hold his glasses tightly to his eyes. The group of five men ran with their heads down directly to the bird and disappeared inside. The whine of the helicopter increased and it lifted off, flying directly at the trees then arcing up and away at the last moment before disappearing into the heavy smoke. All that remained of the men was the dwindling smoke grenade.

"Let's go; we need to move," Brooks said as he got back to his feet. He took off across the field, heading in the direction the men had arrived from. Brad watched as he scouted the ground then found the trail that led into the burning wood line. "This should take us to the garrison area; don't slow down, and stay on me 'til we're clear of the fire," Brooks said. Brad removed his helmet and pulled his balaclava up over his ears and face then watched as the rest of the men did the same thing. Brooks looked back to make sure they were prepped then flashed a thumbs up. "Let's do this," he said, putting his head down and sprinting onto the trail.

Brad followed close behind Brooks, keeping his eyes glued to the trail. They moved quickly, pulling each other along. Fortunately, the trail was wide and because it was lined with already scorched grass, it kept the flames at bay and away from them. Ahead, Brad could see the trail opening into a wide asphalt street. Brooks kept running until they emptied out of the woods and stepped onto the road away from the flames. The wind blew steadily into their faces now, a firm draft being drawn into the fire. Brad pulled the balaclava away from his lips and sucked in deep breaths of the clean air. Grabbing at his combat shirt, he tugged at the collar to pull it down and allow his skin to breathe.

Looking down the street and into the main camp, he could see the now burnt out and skeletal frames of the buildings. The fire had already passed through and took everything with it, leaving only scorched earth. Bodies lay broken and charred in the yards in front of the structures. Brooks didn't allow them to slow down; he turned them into the center of the street and began walking north. Brad fell in near the rear of the formation, keeping Axe to his right. Brooks, Roberts, and Boone formed a triangle at the front.

Brad was feeling the exhaustion creep in; his boots felt heavy on the hot pavement. When he pulled for another sip from the CamelBak, he came up empty. He shook it off and plodded forward. Axe coughed hard and stopped walking until he cleared his lungs. Brad held up to wait for the big man. He slapped him on the back until Axe nodded at him and wiped his face on his sleeve.

"You think they got it?" Axe said.

"What?"

"Those guys, the ones in black—do you think they got the cure?"

Brad pondered the idea. "I hope not, because she wasn't with them, so that would mean... well, it wouldn't be good."

Axe stopped walking and turned to face Brad. "The cure is a she?" he asked.

Brad shrugged. "Yeah, that's what we've been told."

A bright spotlight lit the front of the column then a man called out from somewhere ahead, concealed in the smoke and shadows. "Halt! Who's out there," a voice called.

Brooks stopped moving; he put his hands up and the others followed suit. "Friendlies coming in!" he shouted back. Brooks stayed motionless, waiting for a response.

"Okay, move up, but keep your arms and weapons out," the voice replied.

Brooks held his rifle out and away from his body; he paced forward with Roberts and Boone falling in beside him. Brad did the same and proceeded forward. The spotlight stayed on them, cutting through the heavy gray smoke. As they stepped closer, a fence and gate appeared through the haze. A pair of HUMVEEs with soldiers standing over guns in the turrets slowly materialized. The spotlight drifted behind them and Brad could now see it was mounted atop a Stryker vehicle.

A soldier ran forward and pulled back a section of the gate, allowing them to file in. As they entered, another one looked at Roberts and reached out for him. "Damn, Roberts, where the hell have you been?" the soldier said, stepping forward then looking back to close the gate behind them.

Roberts dropped his hands. "Ah hell, it's good to see you guys."

After securing the gate, he turned and yelled up to the soldier in the Stryker, "It's okay, guys; it's Roberts." The soldier turned back to them. "Sorry about the extra security. We got hit a few hours ago; someone attacked the outpost and things have really gone to shit."

Brad moved to the front. "We were with a patrol south of here that was ambushed."

The man looked at Brad's uniform and the nametape. "Sergeant Thompson?"

"Yeah, that's me."

The soldier's face hardened. "Aww, shit; they've been looking for you. Is that chief with you all too?"

"Chief Rogers? No, he should be here."

The solder turned and yelled back up to the Stryker. "Sir, this is Sergeant Thompson!"

A young lieutenant bounded from a hatch and skidded across the surface of the vehicle before dropping to the ground. The man wore a similar multi-cam uniform; although, his was covered in dirt, grease, and blood. His face showed signs of stubble and his eyes drooped from fatigue. "Sergeant Thompson, the colonel has been looking for you… well, all of us have."

"The colonel?" Brad asked.

The lieutenant's eyebrows lifted, showing surprise that Brad was unaware of who he was speaking. "Colonel Ericson? The outpost commander," he said.

Brad shrugged and lifted his M4, clicking the three-point sling to the shoulder of his gear. "Well, let's go then; I can't wait to debrief him."

Chapter 21

Joe heard the rustling of leaves and forced his eyes open. The thick Appalachian fog settled in on him and made every part of his body shiver from the dampness. The prisoner was grunting again. Joe watched as Dan pulled away the man's gag, fed him more pills, and then poured water in his mouth. The man shook his head, refusing to swallow, so Dan pinched the man's nose and poured in more water until he finally gagged down the pills. Joe watched the older man work on the prisoner; he showed no emotion as he carried out his ugly deeds. The old Marine was business-like, as if he was hanging a picture frame. Not a question of mercy or brutality, he was just performing another task.

Dan allowed the man enough time to catch his breath before replacing the gag and pulling the hood back over his head. The prisoner was already wearing heavy shooter's earmuffs and thick dark-tinted goggles. Dan called it sensory deprivation; he said it was one of the best ways to convince a man to cooperate and force him to rely on his captors. Especially out here, where everything was a threat, the man's own thoughts would scare him more than the reality around him. Since the man had been blinded and deafened, his actions went from defiance to childlike, quickly submitting to them.

The trucks were a treasure trove of information: maps, stolen mail, and pictures. There were boxes of ammo, canned goods, and plenty of narcotics, which the prisoner was currently enjoying. The intel gave Dan a good idea of what they were up against. This was not a group of do-good survivors; they were more of a street gang. Dan referred to them as pests that required extermination.

After the initial contact, Dan gathered the rest of his men and sent them up the mountain after their families. He told them to leave no trail. If Joe and Dan managed to fail, he wanted the strangers' attack against them to end at the cabin. He told them he would get information from the wounded man and take care of Chuck and company — slow them up as best he could then meet them in a day or two.

The wounded man was reluctant at first, but Dan had a way with people and this prisoner was no exception to the rule. The prisoner slowly came around the longer he bled. Dan promised to treat his wounds and give him drugs for the pain if he could lead them back to where Chuck and the others were camped. They had travelled through the night to reach this place. It wasn't much to look at, lying on a muddy slope at the edge of a wooded valley looking down over a cluster of rusted, tarpaper-sided shacks. A tall wooden fence surrounded most of it with chain link in the front section and a tractor-trailer turned on its side covered one end.

Joe watched as the wounded man slumped back against the tree. "How do we even know he's telling the truth, Dan?" Joe asked. "I ain't seen anything move down there; maybe it's empty."

The old Marine looked back at Joe over his shoulder. He was checking the bindings on the prisoner's wrists and ankles. "Well, he's had more than a double share of Demerol and Prozac; I guess he could still be in a mood for lies, but why would he? I have been doing my part to keep him in his happy place. You will find the more drugs you give a man, the less he tends to give a shit. At this point, I doubt he cares much for Chuck and those scumbags at the bottom of the valley."

"Can't we just leave them alone? I mean, hell, maybe they'll never come back up the mountain after the beating they took."

Dan laughed and shook his head. "And maybe unicorns and puppy dogs will take over the free world. You just don't get it, boy. Guys like that always come back, like a wild dog that craves meat. They'll take a beating, but they will continue to return until they get it. I'm sure Chuck brought his people back to lick their wounds. But they will always know there is something up that mountain, and eventually they will go back for it."

Dan let the prisoner fall back into heavy brush then turned and crawled down alongside Joe. They had replaced the shotgun with a pair of mini-14s from the barn. Joe was now wearing a heavy parka and a load-bearing vest weighed down with magazines. Dan was dressed the same except for a large scope on his rifle and the pouches of grenades he carried. Dan lifted his rifle and swept the compound below.

The sun was breaking the top of the mountain, casting an orange glow over the cluster of buildings. "Look there, behind the long steel building… does that look like their vehicle?"

Joe strained his eyes and looked below at the small compound. There was a large one-story building just inside the chain link fence with a large gravel courtyard next to it. The buildings were arranged in the shape of an L; the one-story building being the short leg, then two rows of long, narrow buildings making up the long leg. Just at the back of the buildings, Joe could see a number of vehicles, and one he was sure was the truck.

"That's the truck; I'm certain of it," Joe whispered. "What are we going to do?"

Dan yanked a long strand of grass from the damp ground and chewed at its root. "Well, I was thinking we should take our friend home. He held his end of the bargain and got us here."

Joe opened his mouth to argue when he heard voices coming from below. He turned to Dan and could see from the expression on his face he'd heard them too. Joe held his breath and looked down at the trail below them.

Moments later, a group of men appeared on a previously unseen thin trail just meters below. The lead man, wearing camouflage pants and a gray sweatshirt, carried a crossbow; the two behind were younger and skinnier and, together, they struggled to carry a whitetail deer. A fourth man, farther back, lugged a large burlap bag over his shoulder. The bottom of the sac was red and dripping with blood. Aside from the man with the bow, none carried weapons at the ready.

One of the young men grunted and lost his grip, dropping the front half of the deer to the ground and causing the second man to trip over the carcass. Crossbow turned back and scowled at them. "Come on, dammit, this is taking entirely too long!"

The man in the back moved forward and dropped his canvas sack. "Here, Jeb, take the bag and I'll have myself a spell on the deer."

The young man stared at the bag, then looked up at the older man and nodded. He got back to his feet and hoisted the bag to his shoulder, allowing the other to grab the deer by its neck and lift it to his hip. Crossbow scanned the area and stepped back off down the trail, the others following close behind.

Dan let the strangers move to the bottom of the trail and create separation before he spoke. "That's it, we got the right spot; looks like we caught them on a grocery run," he whispered. "What I wouldn't do for a radio and a C-47 Spooky right now. Good ol' Puff the Magic Dragon would knock these boys outta their socks."

"Dan, what the hell did you do in the Marines?" Joe asked.

"A bit of this… a bit of that," Dan said.

Joe shook his head and pressed his face back into the tall grass. He watched the men navigate the hill and cross a street at the bottom. They casually walked to the chain link fence and removed a bit of chain, letting the others through before latching it behind them.

"Arrogant bastards don't even post a guard," Dan said. "We'll let them get inside, give them a few minutes to get lazy, and we'll follow the trail."

Joe bit his lower lip; Dan looked at him and smiled. "Don't sweat it, kid; this is going to be fun."

Joe scowled as Dan crawled back up the hill; he manhandled the prisoner back to a sitting position, and then forced him up to his feet. Dan dragged the man forward, and then pointed for Joe to move down the trail. "I hope you're right about this," Joe protested.

"I'm always right, 60 percent of the time," Dan laughed.

He stepped off into a controlled slide in the damp grass, dropping down the slope and emptying out onto the trail below. Joe looked up to see Dan pushing the prisoner ahead of him; the man fell hard to his back then half-tumbled ahead as Dan dug in his heels to guide the man to the bottom. The prisoner moaned through his gag but quickly faded back to a low grunt.

Dan shoved the prisoner forward then back to his feet. He pushed him to Joe. Joe clenched the back of the man's shirt in a balled fist and guided him ahead of them. When Dan pointed to the front gate, Joe acknowledged the direction and moved down the trail toward it.

"You sure on walking right to the front door?" Joe said.

"Not particularly. Let me move out ahead of you; if anyone takes a shot at us, leave him where he stands and run to cover. If we get separated, make your way back to the blockhouse."

"Okay, Dan," Joe said. He stiffened his arm and guided the prisoner straight ahead. The man was slumping in his steps, fatigued and staggering from the drugs. Dan moved past them and stopped where the hard-packed trail met the side of the blacktop road. He searched in both directions then ran across. Joe held in place, waiting for Dan to scout the immediate area. Dan pressed his back against the wood part of the fence then ran at a low crouch to the gate. He put his hand to the latch and then looked back at Joe, waving him forward.

"What the hell are we doing here?" Joe mumbled to himself.

He took the prisoner and pushed him onto the road and then, eager to get out of the open, he nearly dragged the man behind him as he crossed. He quickly moved up beside Dan, who grabbed the prisoner by the arm and nudged him gently against the gate. Dan turned and pointed to a gravel parking lot. The lot was filled with several empty vehicles on flat tires, and at the back of the area was a pair of overflowing green dumpsters.

"We'll hide over there while we watch. Get ready to move; this won't take long," Dan whispered.

Joe watched as his mentor handcuffed the prisoner's wrist to the chain link fence. Dan then tied a small bit of wire through the bottom of the gate's frame and laced it along the ground to the corner fence post. He pulled a grenade from a pouch and used a small strip of green tape to fix the body of grenade to the post then took the slack out of the wire and attached it to the pin.

Joe shook his head. "That's dirty, Dan."

"Yup," Dan said. "Dirty Dan, that's what they used to call me."

"You like this shit, don't you?" Joe asked.

Dan looked back at him. He pursed his lips and shook his head. "Nope, I'm just good at it."

Dan pulled the hood from the prisoner's head and removed the wounded man's earmuffs, goggles, and gag. The man looked at Dan, his eyes squinting from the bright light. "Deal's a deal; you showed me the way home, and I brought you here. Try and stay out of trouble, okay?"

With bloodshot eyes and dilated pupils, the prisoner looked through Dan—obviously stoned out of his mind. "Well, see ya around," Dan said before pushing the man against the gate.

Dan drew his 1911 and fired two quick shots into the dirt. Joe, not expecting it, jumped.

"What the hell you waiting for? Run!" Dan shouted.

Joe quickly bounded forward, following the older man to the dumpsters. Together they ran at a full sprint, sliding on the gravel and ducking between the cars and the green dumpsters. Dan pulled the scoped rifle from his shoulder and nestled in under a big truck. Keeping Joe positioned behind him.

Joe pulled his own rifle and went to crawl next to Dan. Dan held up a fist and waved him off. "Just watch my back; if you see something, point it out to me," he said.

It didn't take long for the shouting inside the fences to start. Doors slammed and men yelled obscenities at each other. A man walked into the open, just behind the gate. Barefoot and shirtless, wearing torn blue jeans, he clutched an AR-15 to his naked chest. The man staggered toward the gate then stopped and raised his rifle; he held it for a moment then took his eye off the stock, showing recognition. He lifted his head and yelled to someone out of sight just behind him. "It's that son of a bitch Chris; thought you all said he was dead."

A voice hollered; the sound of it chilled Joe—he knew it was Chuck. "Can't be. I saw Chris take a round to the chest."

The shirtless man stepped forward, his head swiveling while searching the surroundings as he walked. "Yeah, it's Chris alright. Hey, buddy... Chris... it's me. What's wrong with ya?" the man hollered. He stopped again and looked back. "I think he's drunk or something."

"Hold up; maybe he's infected," Chuck said.

Shirtless held his ground, hesitating. More men came into view around him, one far larger than the rest of the group, wearing an olive green jacket, and carrying the MAC-9 at his side. Joe immediately recognized him as Chuck. The man moved into the group, stopping to examine the man standing at the gate.

"You high or something? What the hell's wrong with you, Chris?" Chuck said.

Joe lowered himself to the ground, still keeping the men in sight from his hiding place behind the truck. "The fat one, it's the leader; kill him so we can get out of here," Joe whispered.

"Patience, grasshopper," Dan whispered back.

Frustrated, Joe pushed away, resting on the backs of his heels as he watched the group of strangers. The fat one shoved one of the others ahead of him and the man approached the fence. Joe recognized him as one of the younger men that carried in the deer. Another man stepped to the side, the hunter with the crossbow. He raised his weapon and approached to within feet of the gate then waved the young man forward.

Crossbow froze and then spun, searching the outside. "He's handcuffed!" he yelled.

"What ya mean handcuffed?" Chuck asked.

Crossbow looked back, irritated. "He's handcuffed... not many ways to explain it, Chuck!" he retorted. "Get some bolt cutters."

The young man dropped back and disappeared from view while the others moved forward, gathering around the gate but still staying inside the fence.

Dan adjusted his position, rising up on his elbows and pressing his eye to the scope. "See how they move? This group is used to being in control; even after what happened yesterday, they feel safe. No guards posted, no patrols... even that hunting party with the deer was lightly armed and careless," Dan whispered.

The young man returned carrying the bolt cutters. He stepped up between Shirtless and Crossbow and approached to the gate. Chuck moved up behind them to get a better view. "Cut him down," Chuck said, his MAC-9 still at his side.

Joe heard Dan click the safety off on his rifle. "These guys are really stupid," Dan whispered.

"You sure we need to kill 'em, Dan?" Joe said.

Joe pulled the rifle in tight. "Yeah; if we don't, they will come back up the mountain. I'm not willing to stake Amy and the others' lives on it."

The young man tried to maneuver the bolt cutters through the chain link to get at the handcuffs. Chris—wounded on the other side—was hanging by his arm now, the tension making it even more difficult.

Chuck stepped ahead and pointed at the latch. "Open the gate, dummy; you ain't never gonna cut it from out here."

Shirtless lowered his rifle and fumbled with the gate's latch; he pulled it in and the young man with the cutters stepped out. The posture of Crossbow immediately shifted to panic. "Grenade!" he screamed as the gate's motion popped the pin of the grenade, a tiny spring throwing the spoon free and clanging into the air.

Crossbow stepped back, Dan's rifle barked, and a heavy .300 Win Mag round hit Crossbow square in the chest a millisecond before the grenade exploded and obscured the group in a flash of dirty smoke. Dan shifted his position; rolling from the truck, he fired again into the smoke. He then rose to his knees, firing a third round. Joe searched the gate area but couldn't see anything through the smoke.

Dan got to his feet and grabbed Joe before running through the back of the parking lot and into the dense brush. They climbed into the thick trees partially up the hillside before stopping again.

Dan pointed a finger toward the small trail they traveled earlier. "Keep watching our six," he said as he got back on the scope and searched the gate; he fired again, then again.

"What are you shooting at, Dan? I can't see shit," Joe said.

"Just keeping their noggins down so they can't maneuver."

Screaming from inside the compound intensified and someone fired their weapon, the MAC-9 letting out a long burst. As the smoke cleared, Joe could see bodies at the gate. The wounded man now lay limp, though still attached to the now mangled gate. Shirtless and the young man with the bolt cutters were down—lying together in a lump—and Crossbow was on his back with his legs apart. He searched and spotted Chuck sitting with his back to the building, his left leg twisted oddly. Chuck had a bloodied bandage tied around his knee in a hasty tourniquet.

"There he is… by the building," Joe said.

"I see him," Dan answered.

They could hear Chuck screaming as he raised his weapon and fired another wild stream through the gateway, the rounds harmlessly smacking into the dirt and pinging off the gate. A man peeked around a corner; Chuck turned and yelled at him. The man peeked out again, and then ran to Chuck's side, grabbing his arm, and prepared to drag him when Dan's rifle fired again. The man slumped and fell across Chuck's lap, causing him to scream out yet again. Chuck wrestled with the body and rolled it off him.

Chuck tried to roll away from the wall and crawl to cover; he lay on his belly, grabbing dirt and trying to pull himself away. He barely moved, his broken leg refusing to cooperate. He rolled to his back and looked up at the sky while shouting more orders.

Joe saw movement from farther down the road and tapped Dan's shoulder. Dan lifted up and looked far down the road with his scope. "I wondered how long before they showed up," Dan said.

Joe squinted, looking down the road; he could tell by their movement they were infected. A tall barrel-chested one led the group. More fell in behind the leader; they approached boldly, not stopping. The leader let out a loud moan that echoed up the valley and seemed to excite the others. When even more materialized out of the woods, the mass began jogging then quickly moved at a full sprint, the small group rapidly becoming a horde. Chuck's panicked screams joined the sounds of the approaching pack.

Dan and Joe turned to look back at the group of buildings; Chuck was gone. Dan got back to his feet, turned to climb up the hill then stopped and looked back at Joe. "Let's go; we need to be getting back."

"What about Chuck?" Joe asked.

"I'm sure that'll work itself out; come on, we need to move before the infected get any closer."

Chapter 22

He wiped the dirt and sweat from his face with the back of his sleeve. He was riding in an open-topped HUMVEE—an older model with the soft skin removed. Brooks was in the seat next to him, the other men crammed into the cargo compartment at the back. They were inside a smaller containment area now, full of long grassy fields, located around an airfield. Most of the open spaces now congested with green structures—a newly formed tent city. The outer parts of the camp were designated as hostile; no foot patrols permitted outside the wire, only up-armored, two-vehicle patrols.

Helicopters buzzed overhead, some swooping in low and moving back toward the auxiliary airfield for refueling ops before going back out on missions. The driver slowed as the vehicle passed through a zigzag of barriers and hasty checkpoints comprised of a group of soldiers standing behind strands of barbed wires and sandbags. Just behind them, a battery of field artillery guns sat silent as weary soldiers clustered on the ground, eating meals from plastic pouches. Others removed rounds from tubes and positioned them near their guns.

The young MP at the roadblock looked at the passengers closely then pulled wire out of the way to wave them through. On the other side, the HUMVEE pulled to the side to stop, dropping Roberts, Boone, and Axe to rejoin the others. The goodbye was nonchalant, no hugs or trading of emails. A quick travel safe and a slap on the back, and the trio were off to locate the remnants of their units. Brad wished them well and hoped they would be able to stay safe.

The vehicle pulled off again and parked in a muddy motor pool crammed full of a variety of vehicles. The driver pointed down a walkway made of stacked pallets with green tents positioned on both sides. "Just follow that all the way up. You will find the TOC at the end, which is where the old man is. I need to top this thing off with fuel before they run the tanks dry."

Brooks nodded and stepped away from the military vehicle, throwing his pack over his shoulder and grabbing his Kevlar with a free hand. Brad joined him on the wooden walkway. The sun was creeping up, the heat beginning to burn off the light fog that blanketed the grounds. Generators were running all around, the steady hum mixing with the sounds of aircraft coming and going.

"Feels strange to be back on a camp like this," Brad said.

Brooks looked around and kept his pace. "Yeah, like we're back in the sandbox; some things never change."

Another pair of guards stood at the end of the path. They looked suspiciously at the two mud-and-blood-covered strangers. One held up a hand and approached them cautiously. Brad spoke before the man could ask a question.

"I'm Sergeant Thompson; the colonel sent for me," Brad said.

The man's eyes went wide. "Wait here; I'll let him know you've arrived." The man backed away and disappeared under a tent flap then quickly reappeared with a female lieutenant in a fresh uniform and a butter bar on her patrol cap. "Sergeant Thompson," she said, looking at Brooks. He grinned at her and pointed an index finger to Brad.

"I'm here; can you tell me what this is all about?" Brad asked.

She looked Brad up and down, frowning at his appearance and foul scent. Brad clenched his jaw. "I'd have changed into my church clothes, but I came right from the playground." His tone caused Brooks to chuckle. "Sorry, ma'am — I was under the impression this was important. If you'd like, I could come back later?"

The young second lieutenant rolled her eyes and gave them both a disapproving glance. "Follow me," she said. She turned and pulled away the tent flap, stepping into the Tactical Operations Center. The tent had field tables going all along the walls with soldiers stooped over them, working radios and processing intelligence. At the end of the room was a tall white board with a map of the outpost. As Brad and Brooks moved in, Brad saw Colonel Ericson being briefed by a number of junior officers. They pointed at divided areas of the map where colored status symbols indicated threat levels.

The colonel made eye contact with Brad for a moment then diverted his eyes back to the map, listening to his operations officer. He asked a number of questions then dismissed the men before turning to the young lieutenant. "Is this him?" he asked.

"Yes, sir; they came in on the south perimeter just minutes ago," she answered.

The colonel turned and looked Brad up and down. "How is it out there?"

"It's bad, sir," Brad answered.

"I understand you were with the two-two element when they were ambushed; we've been looking for you for a while now," Ericson said.

"Yes, sir; we were hit just outside of the village. I don't kno—"

"We know about the attacks. Your situation wasn't unique; we were hit by these raiders all over the compound. The perimeter has been compromised; we have Primals in the wire."

"Sir, I—" Brad stuttered.

Ericson paused and took a deep breath, pointing his hand to silence Brad. "Don't worry; that's not why I brought you here. Follow me, Sergeant." The colonel stepped off briskly to the rear of the tent and, lifting another flap, stepped out the back. Brad turned to Brooks, who shrugged and quickly moved out to catch up with the colonel.

When they got outside, the man was already swiftly moving to the airfield with two MPs dressed in full battle rattle flanking him on either side. He stopped just at the edge of the tarmac and waited for Brad to join him at his side.

The colonel turned to face Brad and then shot a knife hand at a large military transport aircraft resting diagonally across one end of the airfield. Two MRAPS and a Stryker vehicle surrounded it. "Sergeant, can you tell me why in the hell this aircraft decided to park in my backyard, and why it is refusing to move until the man on board speaks with either you or Chief Rogers?"

"Sir, I—"

"Well, I think it's time you went and found out."

Brad stood looking at the aircraft, unsure what he was expected to do. He turned and looked at Ericson.

"Sergeant, go find out what they want," Ericson said again, losing patience.

"But, sir… Chief Rogers…? Where is he?" Brad asked.

The colonel softened his tone slightly. "We've located him. Birds spotted him several hours ago in one of the perimeter towers, and we've already sent out a patrol to get him back here. In the meantime, I'd love to get that thing off my operational airfield. These men will escort you on board." Ericson turned to the escorts. "Corporal Smith, make sure these men receive all the support they need."

The two MPs stepped aside; one waved a hand forward, and Brad led the way with Brooks moving next to him. Brad spoke softly without turning his head. "You have any idea what this is about?" he said.

"Not a clue, brother," Brooks answered.

The MP marched them down the edge of the tarmac. "Can you tell me what's going on?" Brad asked one of them. The corporal did not respond; he just continued forward, walking past the Stryker vehicle, and moving along the body of the aircraft to a set of portable stairs leading to an open door. The MP stopped and pointed a hand to the top. At the entrance to the aircraft stood a man dressed in black—same as the ones they'd faced near the school and again on the road—same as the ones who evacuated on the helicopter.

"What's this?" Brooks said, putting up a hand, preventing Brad from stepping closer. He turned sharply to one of the MPs. "Do you know who these men are?" Brooks said, nearly shouting.

The man in black at the top of the ladder stiffened his posture, drawing his submachine gun against his body. Brad hesitated; pulling back, he turned back to the MP. The escort faced him and said, "Look, we don't know what's going on. They landed a few hours ago and refused to allow anyone on board."

"Who are they?" Brad asked.

He looked at Brad, raising his head in shock. "Damn... you really don't know. They are with the CNRT, the closest thing left to a federal government. The colonel isn't really fond of them, so we've backed away from most of their agendas recently."

"So why are they here? You know they probably caused all of this," Brooks said.

The MP looked him in the eye. "The colonel has his suspicions about the attacks, but that's what you're here for. Colonel wants his real estate back and this aircraft moved. Here... you better hand over your weapons."

"They want our weapons?" Brad asked, astounded. "What kind of meeting is this?"

The corporal leaned in. "Sergeant, you give the word and I'll be up those stairs to back you up, but for now we play by their rules."

Brad chewed his lip, not exactly reassured. "Okay," he said. He unclipped his M4 and passed it off to the escort then removed his M9 from the drop holster on his right thigh — neglecting to take the Sigma pistol from the paddle holster hidden in his waistband. Brooks handed off his weapons to the second MP, under the watchful eye of the man in black at the top of the ladder.

Brad turned away from the escorts and moved up the stairs with Brooks close behind him. At the top, they were greeted by the first of the recovery team, a tall man with an MP5 strapped to his chest and a balaclava rolled down around his neck. The man's black sleeves rolled up past his forearms, revealing tattoos and a dive watch. Brad walked past the guard while Brooks stopped to stare him down for a brief second. The man waved them inside and turned them over to a second man in black.

Brad stepped into the fuselage and paused to assess the surroundings. He'd entered near the front of the plane; the seating area was filled with people, all rows occupied with the exception of the first three at the front. The rear cargo area congested with others, including women and children. As Brad's eyes focused in the dark light, he realized some of the people in the cargo area were in mixed uniform. When he recognized his men, Brad's face broke into a smile, and he turned to rush to the rear. Mendez stepped forward with his arms up, moving to the front of the aircraft before quickly being halted by another man in black.

Brad sidestepped the guard next to him, seeing more faces he recognized. Cole, Henry… all his men were there. The guard at the door quickly moved in front of Brad, preventing him from moving to the back.

"What the hell is going on here?" Brad asked.

From the front of the aircraft, a silver-haired man in uniform stepped into the space. Brad turned to the movement and spotted the older man before seeing Sergeant Turner at his side.

"Turner?!" said Brad, his jaw dropping. He lunged past Cloud, grabbing the man in a bear hug. "How...? When...?"

Turner squeezed him, chuckling. "It's a long story, brother. I think you should talk to Colonel Cloud."

Brad looked at the silver-haired man. "Cloud?"

"Good to put a face to the name," Cloud said, sticking out his hand.

Brooks pushed Brad aside. "Ain't you the son of a bitch that left us to die on that oil platform?"

Cloud nodded his head slowly. "Yes... That would be me," he answered. "I'm Lieutenant Colonel James Cloud; I'm in charge here. Maybe you felt abandoned—I understand your heartbreak—but the real world isn't as accommodating as you might want it to be."

Brooks took a step closer, pressing his forehead next to Cloud's. "You left us."

Brad put his hand on Brooks' shoulder, trying to calm him. A guard stepped from the back, dressed the same as the others, and jutted forward a thickly stubbled square jaw. "Can we get this prisoner exchange made and get the hell back to the Mountain, sir?" the man said.

"Prisoner exchange?" Brad said, turning to the man.

The man pushed himself closer. "You do have the girl, right? Get her onboard, and we can drop the gate and unload your people—"

Cloud raised his hand, cutting the guard off. "We haven't gone over details yet, Mr. Walker. If you wouldn't mind standing down with your men, we can work this all out."

Brooks turned on his heels, finding a new target for his frustration. He pushed against the guard so quickly that the man had to take a step back. "So who the hell are these chumps?" Brooks said sternly.

The man showed his teeth in a forced smile, pressing his face back at Brooks. Cloud moved closer and put a hand on Walker's shoulder, easing him back. "This is Mr. Walker and his team; they are... well, they are contractors. They take care of company business."

"Mercs?" Brooks asked.

Walker hissed, "I'm a businessman. Most of you military types ditched your post when the balloons went up. We do the work you're afraid to."

"You're a punk," Brooks snarled. "I've seen your handy work."

"Okay, gentleman," Cloud said, trying to break the tension. "Mr. Walker, if you could give us some space, we can work this out and be on our way."

Walker nodded, keeping his eyes on Brooks. "You've got five minutes then we do this my way." Walker took a step back and walked to the cargo area. He turned around, still shooting Brooks a steely glare.

"You made a new friend," Brad whispered.

"Everywhere I go," Brooks responded, holding his glare on Walker.

Cloud looked to the other guards and pointed to the rear. "You two as well; give us some space," he ordered. The guards shuffled to the back with Walker, standing at the ready and surrounded by the passengers of the aircraft. When Cloud was sure they were out of earshot, he leaned in. Brooks still had his back turned to the group, keeping his eye on Walker.

"We've got a problem," Cloud whispered.

Brad looked back. "What do you mean 'we'?"

Turner casually walked to the side and leaned against an empty seat back; he stretched then looked at Brad. "Seems those contractors think we are here to do a prisoner exchange. Us for some little girl?"

"What?" Brad exclaimed. "Ella?"

Cloud swallowed hard. "Yes, she is an immunity carrier for the virus; she may be a—"

"Old news, sir," Brooks said without looking back.

Cloud nodded. "Right; my boss is in command of the CNRT, a general officer—General Reynolds—one of the last remaining figureheads for the Federal Military, or at least he believes so."

"Never heard of him," Brad said.

"I wouldn't expect you to; he wasn't in a high position when things started. After the evacuation of Washington and as people abandoned the Mountain, high-level officials returned to their home districts; many took sides with other factions and abandoned the idea of the CNRT. Well, that left Reynolds holding the reins. Frankly, the general still has a vision of a central government and refuses to acknowledge installations like this and others located across North America."

"What does any of this have to do with us?" Brooks asked.

Cloud sighed. "The general sent me to collect the remains of your unit, and then make an exchange for the girl. At the time, she was the key to developing a vaccine to prevent further spread of the infection."

"At the time?" Brad asked.

"Yes, things changed. While I was away, the Mountain lab had a breakthrough with Aziz. They have developed something. The general wants the girl removed now, so that only he controls the vaccine."

"So he did all of this, the attack on Savannah, just to kill Ella? Why?" Brad asked.

"Power," Brooks said, still facing the men at the back.

Cloud clenched his jaw and nodded. "Yes, in the simplest of terms, if the CNRT has the sole cure, he thinks they could use it to reunite the factions."

Brad looked at Cloud. "And you think we will give you Ella so you can kill her and have a monopoly on the cure?"

"No," Cloud said.

Turner stood. "He's flipped, Brad. Cloud is with us now," he said. Turner cautiously pulled up the front of his jacket, revealing the pistol grip of an M9. "Don't look… Mendez has one too, and the colonel. We've taken the aircraft; the pilots and crew are restrained. Boys back there just don't know it yet."

Brooks let out an exaggerated chuckle. "Oh boy. So how is this going to work? We've got a cargo bay full of civilians and between them and us, a highly trained crew of assholes."

"Easy… In about two minutes, Walker is going to see us up here bullshitting. In his typical fashion, he will lose his temper and storm to the front and attempt to take charge."

"Then?" Brad asked.

Turner spoke, shifting his position so that he was now just beside Brooks. "We take him and hold him hostage. Mendez will drop the ramp and evacuate the passengers to the field. That will just leave us in a bit of a standoff with Walker."

"They cannot be allowed to leave here, not 'til they pay for Gunner's and Parker's deaths," Brooks said.

"They won't," Cloud said.

Brooks looked over his shoulder at Cloud. "You're not off the hook either."

"Understood." Cloud looked down at his shoulder holster. "I have a weapon. When it happens, take it from me; it's locked and cocked."

Brooks shook his head and lifted the back of his shirt; the H&K MK23 was at the center of his back. "Got my own," Brooks said.

Brad rubbed the belt over his back pocket. "I'm good. Let's do this."

Brooks shook his head at Walker mockingly, and then turned around to face Cloud. He threw up his hands in a frustrated gesture and stepped to the aircraft's door. Walker shouted from the back, "Hey, where do you think you're going?"

Brooks froze and turned back at the contractor who was now charging forward, flanked by two more of the men in black. "This is pointless; I won't be a part of it." Brooks said. Brad looked at Brooks with honest surprise, not understanding what Brooks was doing and feeling left out of the plan.

Walker stepped in fast and close; he reached up and grabbed the front of Brooks' shirt, pulling him in. "You ain't going anywhere," Walker yelled with spittle hitting Brooks in the face. Brooks brought up his right arm between their bodies. His hand gripped the MK23, and he pressed the tip of the barrel into the meaty portion of the man's chin. Brad caught himself up on Brooks' organized chaos; he drew the Sigma pistol at the same time as the second contractor leveled his own weapon at Brooks. Turner quickly moved, stepping behind Cloud and placing his own M9 against the colonel's temple.

Civilians in the back began to scream and huddle. The remaining contractors in black moved forward and raised their weapons at the new threats.

Cloud put his hands in the air, going along with the ruse of being a hostage. "Okay, everyone just calm down. I'm sure we can still make a deal; lower your weapons!" he shouted at the contractors.

The contractors backed away, weapons still raised. Walker stiffened as Brooks pushed the barrel hard into the man's chin, forcing his head to go back and look up at the ceiling. Brooks' left arm hooked Walker's collar and in a smooth motion, he spun Walker around, the pistol now pressed against the base of his skull. "If you want to live, get your men to stand down," Brooks said.

Walker hesitated, fighting the barrel. Brooks shifted his weight and forced the weapon tighter against the man's skull, causing his legs to bend from the pain. Brooks tightened his grip with his left arm. "Your call, Walker; I can end this for you right now," Brooks said. "You'll have nothing left to worry about; I can make all your problems gone with the pull of a trigger."

"Okay, dammit; lower your weapons!" Walker ordered.

The contractors stepped back, lowering their barrels to the deck. Brooks didn't waste any time. "Turner, get your man to drop the ramp, and get these people off."

Turner shouted, "Mendez, go; get 'em out of here."

Mendez turned away from the others and ran along a wall of the fuselage, pushing his way through the civilians. Mendez worked the controls; the ramp unlocked and slowly began to drop. As the seal was broken, light and fresh air spilled into the cargo bay. Civilians, crowded in a cluster, started pushing to the back to escape. The ramp hit the asphalt and the refugees poured out onto the airfield. Military police from the base moved in, raising their M4s and shouting orders for the contractors to drop their guns.

The base MPs continued moving up from the rear of the aircraft, not knowing friend from foe, keeping their weapons trained on all of them. Brad watched as the men in black slowly placed their weapons on the deck and raised their hands in surrender. The MPs turned their attention to Brad. Brad watched as Turner slowly placed his pistol on an aircraft seat in the row next to him. He released the colonel and put his hands in the air. Brad did the same and looked at Brooks; the man's pistol was still firmly pressed into Walker's skull.

"Brooks, what are you doing?" Brad asked.

Brooks ignored his question. "What do you say, Walker? You want to end this now?"

Walker put his hands up, his knees going weak, head moving forward away from the pressure of the barrel.

The two soldiers at the bottom of the ladder charged in, calling off the guards at the back. One took up a position next to Brad. "What the hell is going on in here?" Corporal Smith said to Brad.

"Corporal, I am Lieutenant Colonel Cloud; I have some very important information for Colonel Ericson," Cloud paused and put a hand on Brooks' shoulder. "Have these men detained. Brooks, you can hand over the prisoner now."

Chapter 23

Brad walked into the room. It was painted bright white, had carpeted floors, and chairs that ran along the walls. A table in the center held jugs of water and boxes of food. After the takedown at the aircraft, he was taken away and separated from the others. The civilians and his men from the compound were moved away as a group, while Brooks and Brad were taken away in a van then separated at the entrance of a building located just inside the cleared sectors.

He was allowed to shower and change into a fresh uniform before being led to this room to await instructions. Even though he was going on nearly twenty-four hours without sleep, the cleanliness made him feel refreshed. Brad walked across the carpeted room, lifted a gallon jug of water, and popped the top. He guzzled down a quarter of it then found a seat by the window. He took the jug with him and sat back, relaxing.

The door opened and Brooks walked in. He stopped, looked smugly at Brad, and said, "You too, huh?"

Brad shrugged and took another drink.

"Well, that makes me feel better; thought maybe I was in lockdown," Brooks said. He moved to the center table and dug through the food box, finding a protein bar. Instead of moving to the chairs, he plopped down on one of the tables and took a bite of the bar before lying back.

"So what's next?" Brad asked.

The door opened before Brooks could answer; the second lieutenant from the colonel's tent walked in with another soldier behind her. "Sergeant Thompson, Petty Officer Brooks," she said.

Brad sat up in his chair; Brooks did not move, remaining flat on the table chewing his protein bar with his eyes closed.

"I'm Lieutenant Speirs, aide to Colonel Ericson; sorry about before. I hope the showers and uniforms were to your standards. I was hoping to let you get some sleep before the colonel sent for you."

Brad took another sip off the jug and returned the cap before standing. "The colonel wants to see us?" Brad asked.

She nodded. "Yes. If you could follow me, the briefing room is just down the hall."

Speirs stepped into the hallway, leaving the door open. Brad pushed up to his feet and stepped across the room in front of Brooks. Reaching down, he offered a hand and pulled the man back to his feet.

"Long day, aye?" Brad said.

"Had longer," Brooks said before yawning. "Let's get this over with."

Brad walked just behind Brooks, following Speirs and the MPs down a long, dark hallway. At the end, they were turned, led up a column of stairs to the top floor, and then directly across the hall. Speirs paused outside the door, knocking until she received instructions to enter. She grabbed the knob and pulled the door out into the hallway before ushering them in. Brooks entered the room first, with Brad following close behind. Brad spotted Sean standing at the front next to Cloud and Ericson. Chelsea, Shane, and Villegas were seated in leather chairs around a long, dark, wooden conference table. More men in faded battle dress uniforms—officers and senior enlisted men who Brad had never seen before—were at the far end of the table, hovering over a map.

Brad ignored the others and moved directly to Chelsea; she stood and greeted him with a hug. Joey Villegas rose quickly, reached across, and slapped him on the back. Shane stood and stuck out his hand. "Ella?" Brad asked, returning Shane's handshake.

Chelsea smiled. "She's fine; sleeping just down the hall. They have guards on her." Chelsea dropped back into her leather chair next to Shane. Brad stepped back, putting a hand on her shoulder. "I'm so happy to see you're safe… all of you," he said.

"Sergeant Thompson," Speirs called from the front of the room. Preoccupied with seeing his friends again, Brad hadn't even watched her enter. He noticed the rest of the members of the room were either seated quietly or standing at the sides of the room. Brad let his hand drop to his side and moved along the table, finding an empty seat next to Joey.

Lieutenant Speirs walked to a long whiteboard and pulled down a detailed overlay map of North America. Joey leaned next to Brad's ear and whispered, "Why we here, bro? All seems a bit above our pay grade."

Brad shrugged and turned his attention to the front of the room. Speirs finished pulling down the map then turned to Colonel Ericson and said, "Sir."

Ericson nodded and took a sip from a Styrofoam cup he was holding. He walked to the map, set his cup on a wooden podium, and then stopped and looked to the uniformed men at the end of the table. "Gentlemen, I know it's been a long twenty-four hours for all of us, but we've received some critical intelligence that needs to be acted on right away.

"I hate sending you back into the fray with so little downtime, but I am sure you will all understand why and be able to relay this urgency to your troopers." Ericson pointed across the room. "This is Lieutenant Colonel James Cloud, formerly of the Pentagon's ground intelligence division, now a member of the Joint Chiefs' Combined National Response Team. Cloud is probably one of the few people on the planet who actually knows what is going on.

"Now, we have been out of pocket and ignored down here in Georgia while trying to rebuild, rescue, and recover as much of the population as possible, but we could only deal with things in our reach. Outside of some shaky radio comms and scattered reception, we've been blind to the world outside of this outpost.

"I know it's felt like we've been alone, that nothing is left since Washington fell. Well, the colonel has convinced me otherwise; there is more left and there is still a mission for us… an important one." Ericson turned and called Cloud to the front.

Cloud nodded and moved along the sides of the room, stopping just in front of the map. "I won't bore you all with too many details, but I do feel some background information is necessary. This past summer, a terrorist group known as the Sons of Bin Laden carried out a complex and well-coordinated biological strike. Even though under close observation, they were able to make simultaneous global strikes. As far as we know, there was not a spot on the globe left uninfected by the Primal Virus. And yes, despite our best efforts at containment, they were successful, far more than even they expected to be, and as far as we can determine, many of their own forces were also devoured in the collapse.

"Fast forward thirty days later, ninety percent of the world's population is on the run or living behind walls. Washington fell; the United States is in chaos. Martial law is stepped up. After the evacuation of D.C., the Coordinated National Response Team was formed. Federal military assets, along with leadership from the remaining members of congress, were moved to a bunker complex in Colorado. The CNRT oversaw and provided guidance and resources to help mass population centers.

"I assure you it was a good plan with the best of intentions, but as population centers dwindled so did hope. Many of our soldiers deserted, returning to their families. Members of congress left their posts, moving back to their districts or seeking leadership positions within the remaining governing factions."

A soldier at the end of the table spoke, "Factions?"

Cloud paused and turned to the map. He dropped the colored overlays one at a time. The first transparent page colored Michigan, Ohio, and much of central and northern Wisconsin in blue. "The Midwest Alliance." He pulled another that cast the mountainous areas of Colorado in yellow. "The Greater Colorado Nations." The last overlay coated Texas, Oklahoma, New Mexico, and Arizona in red. "The United States of Texas."

"This is what's left. Anything outside of these shaded areas, including this outpost, was considered off the grid and no support was provided to them. It was the CNRT's version of performing an amputation to save the body… conserving resources to protect the greater good."

"I take it this didn't go over well?" the soldier asked.

Cloud nodded. "No, it didn't. It led to desertions and even a US Navy fleet refusing to return to port when we told them Norfolk was lost and ordered them to report to Texas."

Ericson moved back to the front of the room. "Let's move it along a bit."

Cloud nodded. "With the help of Chief Rogers and his men, we were able to recover vital information to the spread and inoculation of the Primal Virus—we took a prisoner; a patient who had the key to unlocking the virus in his bloodstream. It took us some time, but I recently received word that a cure and the process to make an anti-virus are available. The CNRT has that information; I can get it for you. This outpost has the means and resources to recover the vaccine and deliver it to the factions."

"If we have it, why isn't it being delivered?" the soldier asked.

"CNRT leadership, primarily General Reynolds, is hoping to retain information on the vaccine and use it as a form of currency to pull the factions back under central leadership. He doesn't want the cure getting out; that is why he attacked Savannah."

"What?" the soldier asked, others at the end of the table sounding off along with him.

Colonel Ericson moved back to the front. "We have solid intelligence that the men who ambushed the patrols on the roads and compromised out perimeter were with the CNRT. They had a mission to take out the young girl down the hall. Like the patient the CNRT is holding in the Mountain, the girl's blood holds a key to making a vaccine. Rather than allowing us to develop that cure, General Reynolds chose to destroy it."

"I lost a lot of good men yesterday, sir," the soldier said. "What do we plan to do about it?"

Cloud stepped toward the table. "I can get you inside the Mountain. I can get you the cure… and I can get you the scientist and medical staff needed to replicate it. There are still laboratories and facilities in Texas that we can use—Fort Sam Houston is still up and running. I assure you, we can get this done."

Ericson put up a hand and moved back to the front to stand beside Cloud.

"Gentlemen, I plan to take out the Mountain and do just that. Brief your men and get them loaded out. Every MH60 Kilo we have on hand is being fueled and ready for this operation. Rangers… get your men fitted for battle; there will be another briefing at 19:00. Prepare your questions. You are dismissed."

The men around the table quickly jumped to their feet, the officers rushing to the front of the room, crowding around Cloud and Ericson to ask questions. Ericson walked them to the door and ushered them into the hallway. Brad and the others got to their feet, looking confused and trying to find their own place in the coming mission. Chief moved across the room and stopped at the table.

"Chief—" Brad said.

"Just stand by after the others leave the room," Sean said, walking away.

Chelsea looked at Brad. "Did you know any of this?"

"Just bits and pieces; I mean, it's not all new information, right?"

"No, I guess not," Chelsea said. "They don't expect us to go to this bunker and to Texas, do they?"

"I don't know," Brad said.

Ericson closed the door, the room once again growing quiet with less people in the audience. He moved directly to the table and stood near Brad and the others.

"You've probably guessed it, but there is more," Erickson said. "I wasn't thrilled with having a hundred Afghan nationals dropped on my doorstep this afternoon."

"Sir, I can expla—"

"Don't worry; it's not important. I've already spoken to Sergeant First Class Turner; your people will be cared for."

Chelsea leaned across the table. "Sir, are we going to Texas?" she asked.

Ericson looked back at her and shook his head. "No, but you can't stay here, either. I am closing Savannah. All that will be staying behind is a small contingent to perform rescue and recovery operations; everyone else is being pulled back once I contact Sam Houston."

"Then what about us?" Chelsea asked.

"You, along with the girl and the refugees, will be moved. I have three Chinook helicopters at your disposal. The first trip will deliver you and your men; you'll need to secure the site and once it's safe, we can deliver the rest of the civilians."

"What site?" Brad asked.

Ericson pointed his hand at Cloud. "This was your part of the bargain, you sell it."

"Sell what?" Brad said.

Cloud cleared his throat and leaned over the table. "In exchange for my help taking down the general and recovering the vaccine, I asked for a favor."

"And," Brad asked.

"I want you and your people to relocate to my family's property in West Virginia. I know it sounds insane, but the place is well equipped. It's high in the hills, up steep ground, and on a lake. There used to be a mining camp in the area, so there is plenty of room for everyone from your compound. We know the Primals are thin in the area; it will be safe there."

"Why us, why there?"

Cloud bit on his lip. "My family is there, and I trust you with their safety."

"And if I refuse?" Brad asked.

"This wasn't an offer, Sergeant," Ericson added.

Chapter 24

The pilot walked around the helicopter, inspecting bits and checking off items on a clipboard. "I just want to give you fair warning that I'm not current on the Chinook." Looking at the man, Brad stopped and held his gear in his hand. The pilot turned, seeing Brad's worried face. "Hey, it's okay; I have over two thousand hours on the thing. I'm just not current. Driving CH-47s keeps me fed and out of trouble so I agreed to come out of retirement."

Brad shook his head, walked to the rear of the helicopter, and waited for his men to assemble with all their packed gear. If this mission went correctly, they would not be returning to Savannah. Brad watched as a large, white school bus entered the airfield and turned toward the three parked CH-47s.

The bus pulled up and stopped, its brakes hissing. The side door opened and Joey walked out carrying his heavy rucksack and rifle. He searched left and right. "Where the hell is Chief? And Brooks?" he asked.

"They are going with the Rangers. Colonel asked for their help; they needed shooters," Brad said.

"Then they should have took me," Joey whined then walked off toward the large twin rotor CH-47 helicopter. Brad walked away from the bus, allowing the soldiers to unload. When Turner exited, he stopped beside Brad and smiled as the rest of the men from the compound fell out, along with several of the Afghan guards. Brad caught the eye of Hassan, who stopped and grabbed him tightly; Brad promised they would have more time to catch up on events once they reached their destination. Brad was surprised to see so many Afghans in the group. Turner later explained to him that the men pleaded to be allowed to join the mission. Colonel Ericson saw no reason to segregate them and allowed any who wanted to volunteer.

Brad stood smiling as he watched Mendez and Cole step off the bus; they all embraced in a tight group hug. Brad traded quick greetings with them, avoiding conversations about families, knowing that there was no word from their home base. Mendez had a large family at Fort Benning before their deployment to Afghanistan; as far as anyone knew, Benning was gone now and soldiers had moved to other bases. All over the country, families traveled with them or to different evacuation areas. For now, Mendez and the others had to just pretend everything was okay at home, that their loved ones were safe. At least until they had an opportunity to investigate on their own.

Chelsea was the last off the bus. She was given the option to stay behind with Ella, but she declined, leaving Shane instead. "Must feel good seeing your people," Chelsea said to Brad.

Brad knew that much of Chelsea's unit was gone, most killed on the platform and several others while trying to reach the States. "They're your people too, Chelsea."

She forced a smile. "I know."

Brad walked beside her to the rear of the CH-47. They had three helicopters in their flight. With only thirty personnel in the advanced party, they would split into two helicopters, allowing the parties the ability to split up to support each other, or as a quick reaction force if need be. Brad's team would drop in first to secure a landing site, and then Turner would go in behind him. The third helicopter would stay in orbit, providing cover.

Cloud relayed coordinates of an open recreation area near his family's home; from there it would be a short foot patrol to the ranch property. Cloud showed some concern that if the helicopters tried landing directly on his father's property, his dad might get the wrong impression and try to shoot them down. Cloud said his old man was a bit of a prepper and a recluse. His father only kept a few people on the ranch as farmhands, but he had his suspicions he would take in nearby neighbors, and Cloud knew, of course, that his wife and daughter were there.

He moved to the rear ramp of the lead CH-47 and pushed in along the center. Long benches ran the length of the aircraft and orange cargo netting was fixed to the walls. Men sat on the benches with their rucksacks between their legs, rifles held with the muzzles down. The soldiers were now properly dressed in Army uniforms and new body armor, similar to what Brad was wearing. Their final outfitting he supposed; if things worked out at the ranch, there would be no reason for them to return here.

Brad walked along the center of the helicopter, nodding as he passed his men. He stopped at the front and sat near the crew chief, who was standing in an open window inspecting a machine gun. Brad gave the crew chief a head count and acknowledged they were ready. The man shot a thumbs up and talked into a microphone. The helicopter whined to life, the engines growing louder. The crew chief left the rear ramp deployed and Brad watched as the bird left the ground and circled the outpost. They stayed quiet as the helicopter climbed into the air, the loud noise of the engines blocking out their thoughts. Brad caught a small package of earplugs and stuffed them in his ears to muffle the sounds.

Fires still burned in all directions as the helicopter cut through large banks of smoke and turned northeast toward their destination. He searched the faces of his men; most lay on the benches, heads back, and no looks of anticipation on their faces—these men were spent from the months of being on alert; they had no adrenalin left to give. This was not Brad's first air assault mission, but even he was having trouble getting focused. He looked at his bag between his knees and tried to visualize the gear inside. Going over a mental checklist, he felt the pockets where his ammo and other essentials were stored.

There was no time to rehearse the landing or go over battle drills. No dry runs if they ran into trouble. Brad focused on the faces of the men and tried to let his mind wander to avoid stressing over the things he had no control of. He put his head down and looked at the floor; the sounds of the engines felt soothing. Close to a three-hour flight to reach the mountain region, they were pushing maximum ferry range for the helicopters. Even with extended fuel tanks and splitting the cargo capacity of the helicopters, they were cutting it close. Still, the CH-47s would be required to stop and refuel at a remote location on the return leg—an operation that could prove to be far more dangerous than Brad's mission was.

Brad felt a slap on his Kevlar push his head down; he opened his eyes and looked up into the face of the crew chief. "Five mikes out," he yelled, his mouth inches from Brad's ear. "I'll give you the two clicks out warning. When we hit, you need to unass, pronto. We have no time to loiter, no fuel to waste, do you understand?"

Brad acknowledged the instructions. He tapped the soldier next to him and held up five fingers; the man nodded and did the same, passing it down the line. Brad watched as men pulled their bags tight between their knees and readied their weapons. He searched their faces and saw Chelsea sitting between Cole and Mendez. She felt his stare and looked back at him with a slight grin; she appeared eager to get this done. The helicopter dropped altitude, banked hard, and quickly changed direction. Brad's stomach dropped to his throat as he looked through a port window; all he could see below was a thick blanket of trees.

The crew chief was standing, his head hanging from the gunner's window; he looked back and showed Brad two fingers. The men on the benches saw the same thing and readied themselves. The Chinook flared again; turning sharply, it dropped to just above the trees then made a steep dive and dropped into a clearing. Before the helicopter had stopped moving, the crew chief was walking the isle hurrying them to the back and down the ramp. Soldiers poured out of the back, tossing their bags just off the ramp then continuing to run forward before dropping to the prone position in a semicircle. Brad had just taken two steps off the ramp and dropped to his knee when he felt the down draft of the Chinook taking flight.

The helicopter left a swirling mist of dust and debris as it departed, leaving them in eerie silence. His team lay motionless, allowing the sounds of the forest to return as their ears adjusted to the elements and their eyes adapted to the light. Brad heard the second Chinook; the forest was so thick that the sounds bounced off the dense cover, and he couldn't predict its direction of approach. From behind, he spotted it moving toward them, and then watched as it performed the same maneuver—circling then quickly losing altitude before flaring just feet from the ground to allow the men to spill from its belly. The soldiers departed and disappeared in the knee-high grass as the second CH-47 pulled away. The third made one quick orbit before it too vanished, following the others.

Brad sat on his knees, his head barely visible above the grass. They would wait ten minutes to make sure they were alone. He lowered himself deeper into the grass, disappearing and trusting his point men while he pulled a handset from his pack. Brad knew that Turner would be doing the same on his side of the landing zone. He lay on his belly and consulted his map. Without visible landmarks, he would have to trust they were dropped on target. Just through the woods, directly to their front, would be a small blockhouse and picnic area overlooking a narrow mountain road.

Brad peeked at his watch and lifted his head, taking a quick sweep in all directions. Confident they were alone, he opened the mic and whispered, "Three-Zero, Three-One, over."

"Go for Three-Zero."

"All clear, we are proceeding to the first waypoint, over."

"Roger."

Brad brought his team of fifteen to their feet; they formed a hasty wedge formation and moved to the tree line. Turner kept his group in cover, watching and waiting as Brad and his men moved toward the picnic site. Turner would stay back the entire trip, just out of site, but ready to move forward if support was needed. Other than that, Brad's team was alone. He moved through the tall grass, which quickly turned to mangled and thorny brush. He swam forward through it, breaking into the tree line.

He lowered his hand and heard the swishing of grass and brush behind him go silent. He knew his men dropped out of sight when he'd signaled. Far to his right, he saw Cole kneeling alongside a tall tree. Brad nodded his head, and Cole stepped into the opening of the picnic area. Just as described, it was a long narrow park with a slim trail running down the middle. Rotting picnic tables were on both sides and a partially collapsed log cabin sat near the entrance, some sort of commemorative plaque on a timber post near its base. Cole moved slowly along the picnic tables; following the road around, he moved next to the blockhouse then paused before waving the others forward.

Brad got to his feet and rushed ahead, falling in alongside Joey as they moved to join Cole. They waited together at the blockhouse as the others moved out of the landing zone and joined them in the park. Soldiers stayed behind, providing security while Brad quickly consulted his map. He drew a line with his finger and indicated the direction of travel to Cole and Joey before sending them ahead on point. Brad found Chelsea and she moved up beside him. They stepped off, following the point men and watched as the rest of the team did the same, forming two columns on each side of the road as they wound down the steep terrain to the mountain trail below them.

Brad quickly relayed instructions back to Turner over the radio, letting him know they were moving to the next waypoint. At the bottom of the road, Cole stopped and waved Brad forward. The mountain trail showed signs of travel and a fight. He silently pointed to spent shell casings, a clear blood trail, and farther down the road to where there was lump in the center, probably a body.

"You want me to run down and check it out?" Joey whispered.

Brad shook his head. "No, best to keep moving."

"Thought it was supposed to be all clear up here?" Cole asked.

"It's supposed to be. Keep moving," Brad said.

Cole nodded and looked to Joey; they stepped off together and made the right-hand turn following the pass farther north. The road was heavily rutted and filled with muddy prints from recent travel. The sides of the footprints were still firm with moisture and not dried or crumbling, making them recent. No distinction between living or Primal to speak of, but it was apparent by tire tracks that trucks had traveled on the gravel road within recent days.

As they moved forward, Brad saw no signs of life but continued searching the dark forest on both sides of the road for threats. Chelsea stayed close to him, covering his flank. Brad turned and looked back, observing as his soldiers patrolled closely with their Afghan counterparts. Mendez stayed farther to the rear to help keep the men from getting too spread out. All on the same team now, they moved together, pointing things out in the distance and helping with maintaining their patrol distance.

It didn't take long for Cole to call the column to a halt. Brad traveled to the head of the formations and joined his men. Piled brush was moved and scattered to reveal a turnoff that led deeper into the woods and up to higher ground. A pile of mangled fly-covered bodies lay in a depression at the shoulder of the road. Brad looked at them and turned to Joey, who'd just walked away from the pile.

"Primals, by the look of it; took a lot of gunshot to bring 'em down," Joey said.

Brad nodded, starting to sweat as the mission became more dangerous.

He looked at his map; Brad knew the turn off was the approach to the Cloud family farm. He made the decision to go ahead with only Chelsea and Joey, holding the others back. He wanted to approach the gates in a small patrol so as not to startle any guards or someone hiding. The others halted and formed a small security perimeter at the base of the drive. He passed instructions back to Turner, who was traveling the road just a few minutes behind them and would hold in place, ready to move up as a quick reaction force if needed.

They walked in a square, Joey beside him, Cole and Chelsea behind him, slowly moving up on what was quickly showing more signs of a fight. Another Primal body lay in the grass, then a man with a shotgun blast to his shoulder.

"Sure this is a good idea, boss?" Joey asked. "I mean, just walking up all casual like this?"

"No—as a matter of fact, I don't," Brad said.

They approached the rear of an old blue pickup truck, the front windshield shot out. Bullet holes cut through the side fenders. Brad held the others back as he walked up along the side of the vehicle and looked into the empty cab. Behind it, another truck followed a long, tubular steel gate blocking the road ahead. The air was damp and swampy from the heavy trees holding in the decaying moisture of the forest floor. There was a subtle breeze dissipating a heavy smell of death, the stench instinctively raising Brad's alert lever. He walked forward around the front of the truck and heard a shout.

"Stop where I can see ya!"

Brad froze and held his hands in the air, allowing the rifle to hang from its sling.

"It's okay; I'm with the Army. Colonel Cloud sent us," Brad said.

"The Army, you say?" the man replied. Brad watched as a skinny rag-covered man stepped from the shadows alongside the gate. Dressed in canvas pants and a flannel work shirt, he stepped into the open, his right hand holding an AR15, his left scratching at his beard.

"That's right, we're with the Army," Brad repeated moving to where the man could see him clearly. Another man stepped into the open, dressed similar to the first but carrying a pump shotgun and had a bandana wrapped around his forehead. The men walked to the steel gate and waved Brad ahead.

"Hell, we ain't seen much of anyone up in these hills," the bandana man said while the first continued to scratch at his beard.

"You okay?" Brad asked the scratcher.

The bandana man laughed, smacking scratcher on the back. "Lice" he said. "Everyone's got 'em."

Brad subconsciously took a step back, causing both of the men to laugh. "Hell… ain't nothin' to be a-scared of," Bandana said, watching Brad step away. "Chuck is gonna make a run into town and get us something for it once things settle down again."

Brad heard a branch snap behind him. The two guards raised their weapons, and Brad turned to see the rest of his group approach the truck. Joey and Cole stepped out to the side while Chelsea stayed just behind them.

Scratchy's chin lifted. "That a woman you got with ya?"

Brad ignored the question. "I'm looking for a man. Dan Cloud; is he here?"

The two guards looked at each other; one pulled the other back so Brad couldn't hear what was said, then he looked back at Brad. Bandana turned back while Scratchy jogged up the road. "We gonna go get Chuck; he's in charge. He can tell you best about Dan."

"Is Dan here?" Brad asked again.

"You should just talk to Chuck. He's a soldier like you all, and you'll like him," the man said.

Brad stood waiting; he pulled the mic from his shoulder preparing to speak.

"Whoa… what's that?" the man asked, pointing at the radio hand mic.

"Just giving my people an update. I have a whole lot of soldiers down on the road waiting to move up."

"I think you best wait before you go doing that. This is our place; we might not find you all welcome."

Brad nodded, letting the radio mic hang at his shoulder. He turned and saw that Joey had moved a bit to the left, better positioning himself. Cole was doing the same on the other side. With Chelsea now perched alongside the fender of the truck, the group formed a small defensive triangle, putting themselves within a quick leap of cover.

Brad saw Scratchy jog back down the driveway; more men followed him, and a fat man moved slowly behind, badly limping from a poorly bandaged leg wound. Brad reached at his chest, pretending to adjust a strap while the others' attentions were focused on the limping fat man. Brad slipped a hand to the radio pouch and muted the volume of his radio, while hot mic-ing the transmitter. It opened the channel so Turner would be able to listen in on their conversation.

The fat man limped ahead while the rest of his party spread out behind him. Every one of them filthy, dressed in rags, and carrying weapons in their arms. The fat man got to within a few feet of the gate. Brad could already hear his heavy breathing and see the man's forehead beading with sweat. The man stopped and looked Brad up and down; his eyes drifted, searching the rest of Brad's group, then locking on Chelsea to linger a bit too long.

Brad spoke, breaking his stare. "I'm Sergeant Brad Thompson. I'm here looking for Dan Cloud."

The fat man coughed then grinned. "Well, hell; it is the Army! I was in the Corps myself—"

"Chuck was Special Forces, Recon Marine," Scratchy said excitedly.

Chuck grinned and nodded at Scratchy. "So, what brings you up to my place?" the fat man asked.

"Like I said, I'm here to see Mr. Cloud. I have word from his son."

The fat man coughed and spit at his feet then looked back at Brad. "Well… you may as well give the information to me then; the man you're looking for isn't here. I live up here with my friends. Cloud isn't here no more. If he comes back, I'll pass it on to him."

"Looks like you all had some trouble. I saw the bodies," Brad said.

Chuck nodded. "Yeah, bunch of guys come up here and attacked the gates. We took 'em out though; killed 'em right in their trucks," Chuck said, pointing at the disabled vehicles. "We tracked them into town… ran into some of the infected… had to turn back, haven't heard from 'em since."

Brad watched the expression of Scratchy and Bandana as Chuck told his story. Bandana looked off into the trees avoiding eye contact, while Scratchy smiled showing rotten teeth, his dirt-caked fingernails continuing to dig at his lice-infested beard.

"You were attacked?" Brad asked. "You know where they came from?"

Chuck nodded and coughed. "Yup, two days ago. And nope, probably one of the groups down the mountain; lots of bad folks down that way," Chuck said, getting a giggle from Scratchy.

"Mind if we go up and take a look at the house?" Brad asked.

"And what exactly would you be looking for?"

"Just quick look around, see if there's anything we might be able to do for you. I have a convoy of trucks down on the road, food, water, supplies, ammo… things to help you out. Medicine for that leg," Brad bluffed.

Chuck used his sleeve to wipe the sweat from his forehead. "Well… I guess a look around won't hurt," he said. "Go on and open the gate."

The fat man stepped back while Scratchy snaked a chain around the rail and Bandana pulled the gate open. Brad turned while waving the others forward; he moved around the gate then stopped at the front. Chelsea passed through the entrance behind him, squeezing around the men; Scratchy reached out and touched her hair. Chelsea spun quickly, catching Scratchy in the teeth with the buttstock of her rifle. The man's lower jaw seemed to explode with blood as the man tumbled back. The rest of Chuck's group burst into sadistic laughter at the display.

"Hell, she's a feisty one," Bandana chuckled as Scratchy writhed on the ground clutching his jaw.

Joey rushed up behind Chelsea. Moving through the gate, he pressed his elbow deep into Bandana's diaphragm, causing the man to gasp as he leaned back against the railing. "She's a Marine and you better treat her like it." He scowled, his eyes cutting into Bandana.

Bandana chuckled nervously while trying to back away.

"Okay, enough of that. Bo didn't mean nothing by any of it," Chuck shouted over the others. "Let us move this conversation up to the house, so I can see what you all got to offer me." Chuck turned away from the group and began limping back up the narrow driveway. Brad waited for the others to move out before he stepped ahead. Two of Chuck's men lingered by the gate, holding off so they could fall in behind Brad.

Joey moved close to Brad and spoke softly, "What you doing, bro? This group ain't right; we should be turning back."

Brad turned his head so that he was looking at Joey but speaking into the open mic. "Hey, we'll just move up to the house and take a look around. I'm sure Turner is someplace close if we need him. He'll know he can't just walk up the driveway."

Joey caught the change in the infliction of Brad's voice and pursed his lips in recognition. "I gotcha, bro. Just stay loose; something ain't right."

The road wound up the hill to a regal log cabin; beyond that stood farm buildings typical of any place Brad had seen in the Midwest. The place fit the surroundings, but the men occupying it did not belong. A flagstone walkway led up to a long covered front porch that ran the length of the cabin. Brad saw Chuck already at the railing. A man beside him moved up the steps and dropped heavily into a porch swing. At one end of the porch was a pile of broken furniture and suitcases full of spilled luggage and belongings. Brad turned the corner and walked up on to the porch; he stopped short of the last step and examined the pile.

"What's all of this? Are those children's clothes?" Brad asked.

Standing near a hand-carved door, Chuck paused and looked back. "Oh, that stuff. Yeah, place is full of it; we cleared it all out to make room. Ain't no women and kids here so not much point in holding onto such things." Chuck pushed in the door, allowing his guards to enter first, then waved a hand at Brad and ushered his group inside.

They entered a large formal family room. Expensive furniture was awkwardly arranged around a large wooden coffee table that had food cans and dirty dishes scattered across it. Chuck pointed to a high-backed chair and asked Brad to sit. Brad moved into the room; he paused to look around while Joey stepped just inside the door and moved to the right, taking up a position with his back to the wall. Cole moved just past him and stopped. After Brad watched his men settle in, he continued to the chair and sat, Chelsea stopping just behind him. Brad saw she held her weapon at the ready.

The living room opened into a kitchen that featured a long wooden lunch counter and bar near the hallway leading further into the cabin. Brad spotted a tall and dark mustached man leaning against a column, a rifle resting in his hands. The man did not move—he just watched. Chuck walked around the table and dropped into an overstuffed leather sofa. He dug through a pile of blankets and removed a half-filled bottle of bourbon; Chuck then removed the cap and took a long pull. He went to pass the bottle to Brad.

"Sorry, I'm on duty," said Brad, putting up a hand and waving it off. "So Chuck, you didn't tell me how you acquired this property."

The fat man's mouth went tight; he turned and passed the bottle to a man who had stopped just by his shoulder behind the sofa. "Huh?" Chuck coughed into his sleeve then spit onto the hardwood floor between his scuffed and worn leather boots. "It's a family place," Chuck said.

Brad looked at the man over Chuck's shoulder; he held a large nickel-plated revolver in crossed arms, a finger on the trigger. The man did not move his head, but his eyes continuously shifted between Joey and Cole. The man at the counter seemed less interested; he moved, sat on a stool at the lunch counter, and placed his rifle across its surface to light a cigarette.

"I was told I could meet a man here; his name is Dan Cloud. How do you know him?" Brad asked.

Chuck shifted uncomfortably. "My uncle."

"And he just left?" Brad asked. "Did he say where he was going?"

Chuck shook his head. "Nope, just left. Listen… these supplies you got, are they close?" Chuck asked, his tone changing.

A gunshot came from outside, followed quickly by another, then rapid-fire blasts from a shotgun. Chuck's guards ran to the window; the man at the lunch counter jumped to his feet and rushed forward. Brad gripped his rifle and pushed back away from the chair.

"What the hell is this?" Chuck yelled, staggering to his feet. "Is this you?" he asked, pointing a finger at Brad.

Chelsea moved over to Brad with her rifle at the ready, Joey and Cole immediately doing the same. The guards were looking out the windows, searching for targets, not seeming to take the soldiers in the room as a threat. Brad grabbed the radio; as soon as he cleared the channel, he heard Turner's panicked voice. "Three-One, Three-one, are you in contact? Over!"

Brad clicked the mic. "Negative, three-zero, it's not us."

Brad looked at Chuck; the man turned away then looked back. "It's probably the same attackers. They're back!" Chuck said.

A front window exploded, knocking back the mustached man and leaving a dark hole seeping blood from his chest. The second guard knelt in front of the window and fired his shotgun, racking off rounds. Joey moved away from the wall and grunted, "To hell with this." He leveled his rifle and shot the man with the nickel-plated revolver then turned and killed another guard against the far wall. He walked back to the center of the room, rushing at a dazed and confused Chuck. Joey stopped and pivoted hard, clubbing the man in the head with the stock of his rifle, knocking him unconscious. "We ain't got time to mess around with this fat bastard. If whoever out there is against him, then I'm on their side."

Joey turned away from Chuck and ran to the door; he flung it open and dropped against the open door frame, firing in the direction of the gate. Cole looked at Brad for instructions. "Go... backup Villegas," Brad said.

Brad walked toward the body of Chuck and flipped the man over to his belly. Ripping a long piece of fabric from the man's shirt, he bound his wrists then rolled him to his back. He told Chelsea to watch him then he grabbed the radio and said, "Three-Zero, we need you."

He turned and ran to the porch; Chuck's men were dead at the bottom of the stairs, more near the gates. Brad saw Scratchy running for a tree line; a loud gunshot echoed and Scratchy slumped heavily to the ground. Cole and Joey stood close to one another, walking the drive while kicking dead bodies. "Where are the shooters?" Brad asked, searching the distant tree lines and shadows.

"I don't know, but they ain't shooting at us," Joey said.

The gunfire stopped, all of Chuck's men lay dead on the ground or bleeding out. Brad joined Joey and Cole in the driveway. He could not see anything; whoever did the shooting was a pro.

"There," Joey said, pointing. In the distance, from between the barns, two men walked toward them with their arms held over their heads.

Chapter 25

The two men walked down from the barns, the sun to their backs causing Brad to squint into the light. His radio squawked; Brad quickly grabbed it. "Get up here, the farm is clear," he said then dropped the hand set. He kept his eyes on the men. One, carrying a heavy barreled scoped rifle, appeared to be in his mid to late sixties. A faded, olive green cap with a black Marine Corps logo stamped on it covered his head, and he wore a dark, tiger-striped parka. The man next to him was younger and stockier; he wore blue jeans with a camouflage shirt and had a rifle slung over one shoulder and a club in his right hand.

"I should have shot you down just for consorting with those scumbags," the man said, stepping closer. "But seeing as you captured their attention for me, I'll give you a moment to explain yourselves."

Brad watched as the square-jawed man walked into view; he immediately picked up the resemblance to Colonel Cloud. "Dan Cloud?" he asked.

The man paused and looked at Brad. "Say again?"

"Are you Dan Cloud? I have a message from your son."

"James? He's alive?"

Brad nodded his head and searched his breast pocket for the envelope. He quickly retrieved it and crossed the open space to hand it to the old man. He tore the end from the envelope then read the handwritten note. He turned his back to Brad while he finished then looked back. "Is he safe?"

Brad clenched his jaw. "He was the last time I saw him, sir. He has things to take care of, then he will be joining us here."

The man nodded. "I understand." Dan looked toward the cabin and stepped off heading to the porch. The younger man moved closer to Brad and extended his hand. "I'm Joe-Mac. Sorry about him; it's been a long couple days," he said.

"What happened here?" Brad asked.

Joe looked around, and then up at the cabin, taking in the broken windows and debris on the porch before looking back at the bodies in the yard. "They came a couple days ago, asking to trade, but obviously looking to steal from us. We ran them off… chased them into town. Dan thought we had them beat, that we would never see them up here again, but they came back. They led some of those infected things up here with 'em.

"We've been hiding out up in the hills, waiting for our chance. Guess when you all came along it was the perfect distraction to start something," Joe-Mac said.

"Is there anyone else? The colonel said his wife and daughter would be here."

Joe-Mac smiled and nodded. "Yes, sir, Dan had them all relocate up the mountain to the lake. There are five families with us."

A man's scream from inside the cabin took Brad's attention; he turned in time to see Dan dragging Chuck through the front door and down the porch steps by his bad leg. Chelsea was following close behind with wide eyes. Dan dragged the fat man to the center of the drive then dropped his leg. He reached down and grabbed him by the back of the shirt.

Joey walked forward and looked down at him. "So… you say you're a Marine, huh?"

"Yeah, yeah, I'm one of you guys. What the hell, man?" Chuck whined.

"You don't look like a Marine," Joey said.

Dan circled around him then squared his feet. He pulled his knife and poked at the leg wound, causing Chuck to scream. "Let me introduce myself; I'm retired Master Gunnery Sergeant Dan Cloud."

Chuck opened his mouth to speak but Dan held up a hand to silence him. "I think you lied to those people to get them to follow your sorry ass." Dan paused and looked up at Joey next to him. He turned and watched Chelsea move down the porch steps; she walked to Chuck and stopped just feet from his head. Dan saw their nametapes. "Now these two individuals here… they are Marines; you are not."

Chuck whined and went to speak again; Dan turned to Joey and said, "Corporal, gag the prisoner."

Joey grinned. "Roger that, Master Guns."

The young Marine lunged forward and dropped a knee to Chuck's chest, pressing him tight to the ground. Chuck squirmed and yelled, protesting while trying to roll away before Chelsea dropped down to assist. Joey pulled a roll of dark green tape and quickly wrapped it around Chuck's head, pulling back the skin of his abundant cheeks, leaving his mouth agape. Chuck wiggled a hand loose; it fell to his hip then came back up holding a small buck knife. He swung it up at Joey, who quickly arched back, the blade cutting the front of his uniform shirt. Chelsea reached out and caught Chuck's wrist. She twisted it, but the man fought her so she twisted it more and plunged it down, watching the blade sink into the fat man's chest.

Chelsea quickly released the handle and backed away. Joey stood up pulling away his uniform blouse, seeing the thin cut through the fabric that barely missed his skin. Chuck squirmed and twisted, squealing through the gag; his blood-soaked hand slipped on the blade while trying to remove it from his chest. Joey stepped ahead, leaned over Chuck, and shouted, "Callate el osico gordota… You cut my damn shirt!"

Dan looked at the bleeding man with disgust, and then glanced over at Brad. "You have a medic?"

Brad shook his head. "No, he isn't with us."

Dan nodded. "Neither do I." The old Marine turned away from the prisoner and walked closer to Brad. "My son… he said you have more friendlies to bring in. I can't give you the coordinates to the lake. You need to do it soon; it's two days to get there and I want to get moving."

Brad looked at him. "Sir, you could give me the lake co-ords and I'll have the refugees flown directly there."

Dan shook his head. "Nope, James said to keep the location secret, so it's this way or not at all."

They heard commotion at the gate and saw the rest of the men walking up the driveway. Turner was double-timing it to get to the front. He stopped and looked down at the prisoner—no longer moaning and kicking—then up at Brad. "Everything okay here?" he asked.

"It is now," Brad said.

He dropped his pack, fished out the satellite phone, and dialed the number. Instead of reaching a person, he locked onto an automated voice message system. Brad left a coded message that told Cloud everything was okay and to send the rest of the people. He disconnected the phone and removed the battery before storing it in his pack.

"Now what?" Joe-Mac asked.

"Now we wait," Brad said.

Chapter 26

Hunched into a jump seat at the rear of the aircraft, Sean sat wearing a mask. He breathed in pure oxygen, which pushed the nitrogen from his blood. A single red bulb sat just above his head, a weak source of light in the blackened-out aircraft cabin. Brooks and Cloud were next to him. They wore black jumpsuits and parachutes like his, heavy gear bags at their feet. This would be Cloud's first high-altitude jump on a real mission. The colonel assured Sean he was qualified, and Sean hoped he was telling the truth because if the colonel burned into the side of the mountain, the mission would be scrapped and all of their asses would be in the wind.

Sean's team was going in ahead of the Ranger elements. They needed to clear the rear access to the bunkers, a secret approach only used when traveling to the remote airfields and maintenance roads. Cloud said the doors were an afterthought in the Mountain's construction design and only lightly monitored—possibly not monitored at all as the Mountain's operational manning rates dwindled. Desertion was a problem at the military site; with the Mountain being in such close proximity to a safe area in Colorado Springs, many of the bunker's inhabitants had chosen to flee.

The unguarded rear lock required dual authentication to open before they would be able to enter the maintenance locker. From there, it would be a short walk to a control room. Cloud would unsecure the magnetic locks on the blast gate, allowing the Rangers access to the Mountain. The only unknown was whether or not Cloud's credentials still work.

When the colonel dropped communications with the general, they turned off the aircraft's transponders and killed the comms uplinks. He hoped the general would believe they were all dead in a crash when they did not check in and the plane failed to return to base. With things more important happening, the hope was the general would fail to update a dead man's security access.

Sean looked left across the seats where Brooks sat with his head back, breathing deeply on the mask, his eyes unseen behind the goggles. Cloud was leaning forward, his legs shaking in anticipation of the jump.

Sean felt his own anxiety building as his eagerness to start the mission squeezed at his chest and back muscles. Cloud said once the evacuation alarms sounded, most would flee the complex without question. The staff, being in no condition to fight anyone, would run or stand down if the opportunity presented itself. He hoped he was right; Sean didn't have the stomach for killing the US servicemen operating the bunker.

A jumpmaster stepped from across the fuselage and stood Sean up; he moved his hands over his gear, checking his equipment and straps. He spun Sean around and slapped his backside before moving to Brooks, then Cloud. Sean began to feel the adrenaline loading his system, and his hands began to twitch as he took in deep breaths of the 100 percent oxygen.

They were all on their feet, the rear ramp opened and locked. The jumpmaster flashed ten fingers and ushered them to the back. He stepped back against a handhold and pointed at his watch then waved them on. Sean stepped forward at a casual walk and jumped into the dark night sky, knowing the others would follow close behind him. He looked down and saw nothing but black; none of civilization's lights—just a dark forest and peaks of cold granite.

Sean arched his back, holding his arms and legs out. He held his breath while guiding his descent, glancing at his watch, and checking the altitude. From the corner of his eye, he could see Brooks and Cloud in a tight formation on his right side, IR beacons attached to their ankles glowing softly in his night vision optics.

"Well, hell… the colonel knows how to jump," Sean said over the internal radio.

"But can he land?" Brooks asked.

"Cut the chatter boys," Cloud responded.

Sean checked his GPS and made a slight adjustment to his glide path. At just above one thousand feet, he reached back and deployed his chute. He felt and heard the snap of deployment as his body pulled against the harness in a sudden deceleration. Looking down, he could see the tops of thick Colorado spruce trees seeming to rush at him through the green vision on his night vision optics.

He searched for an opening, finding only small spaces between the treetops; he flared his chute and pulled hard as his boots hit the ground running. Sean dropped quickly and released his harness, pulling and folding it in as he gathered the fabric. Quietly, he ran to the base of a large Douglas fir where he slipped out of the jumpsuit, revealing the dark woodland camouflage uniform underneath. Sean quickly buried his unneeded gear in a thick bed of needles.

Kneeling alone and in the dark, Sean expertly guided his hands over his weapons and equipment. He looked down again at his GPS; even with many satellites down, he was able to get enough of a signal to navigate. He smiled at himself; he'd done well and only a couple hundred meters from the rally point. He scanned his surroundings and, once confident he was alone, stepped off into the darkness. The trees overhead were thick; the heavy limbs blocked sunlight from reaching the forest floor, allowing heavy growth of weeds and brush to accumulate, so it made for easy maneuvering.

Sean walked along the soft needles, pausing often to drop low into a squat to listen. Occasionally, he heard the breaking of a branch or the hoot of an owl. Cloud told them that Primals were known to be in the area, but there were other predators as well — packs of wolves, bears, mountain lions, and of course, the occasional man in black. He heard the loud snap of a branch and the crackle of dry leaves to his front. Sean held his breath and focused his eyes, locking in on the movement. He could tell by the man's posture that it was the colonel. Sean made a slight hiss with his teeth and watched Cloud freeze.

He moved up behind him and whispered, "It's me — Chief."

Cloud turned back and tossing up an exaggerated wave, pointed at the GPS on his wrist then pointed a finger skyward to indicate going up the side of the Mountain.

"Am I late?" he heard Brooks whisper from behind.

Sean turned back, spotting the other SEAL as he moved alongside Sean and knelt down to wait.

"Everyone good to go?" Sean asked.

The men nodded and Cloud stepped off, leading the way.

They climbed out of the brush and onto a limestone path a half hour later. Moving slowly along a half-poured concrete wall, Cloud crept along then stopped at one end before turning back to face the others.

"There are closed-circuit cameras on the other entrances, but not here. The original plans show this maintenance locker being sealed once construction was completed. Thanks to budget cuts, the bunker was never finished, so this locker remains open to access cable runs and electronic spaces from the service roads," Cloud whispered.

"You sure it's empty on the other side?" Brooks asked.

Cloud nodded, dug through a pouch on the chest of his gear, and removed a small key card then flipped up his NODS. "I'll go ahead to the lock. It uses an RFID chip; once I wave my badge, I'll have to enter my code and submit a retina scan. There is only room for one of us in the locker, but once you hear the door pop, we need to be inside quickly; if the door stays open more than thirty seconds, an alarm will sound."

"Let's do it," Sean said.

Cloud moved ahead; Sean watched as he followed the half-wall to a nearly invisible, narrow passage where thick conduit ran along the base. Sean heard Cloud's boots scrape on the dry earth, then an audible click.

"Come on," Cloud said from the dark.

Sean and Brooks left the cover and scrambled forward. They moved into the narrow passageway, finding Cloud at the end with his hand on a lever, holding open a heavy pneumatic door. He waved the SEALs past him and into another dark space ahead. Clearing the door, Sean led the way in, his feet sliding on the smooth concrete floor. He heard the door ease shut behind him with a hissing noise as gasses escaped the pistons. The door clunked and made a scratching noise when it sealed shut.

The room was beyond dark. With no ambient light to feed his goggles, Sean reached up and activated his infrared headlight, the illuminator filling the small space with invisible light. Brooks quickly moved across the space to the only visible door and dropped into a crouch. His teammate had both hands on his suppressed MP5 and was looking down the barrel. They were in a small concrete-encased room, maybe eight feet wide and ten feet long. The room was void of objects except for a keypad near the now sealed door. A think bundle of cable ran along the ceiling, passing by large fluorescent lights that hung above.

Cloud followed Sean's stare up at the dead lights. "All non-essentials have been powered off. Most of the complex is dark," he said.

"Sounds dreamy; you mind giving us the VIP tour," Sean said.

Cloud nodded and Brooks shuffled ahead to the only other door; pulling down on a latch, the door opened out on well-oiled hinges. Brooks moved through the opening, with Sean trailing close behind, his boots nearly sliding on the dry concrete floor. The concrete dust felt loose and gritty under his feet, as if it were, instead, a layer of talcum powder. Sean came out into the empty corridor, soft bits of light glowing in his goggles; he powered them down and lifted the eyepiece away.

He was standing along the wall of a long tunnel hundreds of feet long. More spaced-out fluorescent lighting blocks hung from the ceiling, every fifth one powered on, providing just enough light to see the floor. The hallway appeared completely deserted. Sean stepped forward, his boots scratching on the dry concrete. He moved into the thickest shadows and dropped to a knee, keeping his weapon ready and waiting for Cloud to move up behind him. Brooks crossed the hallway and found a spot a few meters back, covering their rear.

Cloud stepped to the front and walked ahead, crouched over, keeping his left shoulder close to the tunnel wall. After moving nearly a hundred yards and passing several closed doors, he stopped again, dropped to his knee, and waved Sean toward him. Cloud's hand pointed to a door on the far side of the passageway; the door, unlike the others, showed a small sliver of light escaping from its frame.

Without being instructed, Brooks silently moved ahead and posted outside the door; Sean fell in just behind him. The door shared a similar metal latch, but unlike the locker door, there was a small keypad above the latch. Cloud again removed his keycard and readied it by the door. Cloud ran his badge over the door, the keypad lit in green backlighting. He entered the code and the door clicked. Brooks moved ahead, nudging Cloud out of the way; he tilted the handle and swung into the brightly lit room, leading with his suppressor.

Sean pushed in behind him. The room was the size of an average one-car garage and stank of ozone air and body odor. A bank of black and white monitors was mounted on the left wall. Just below them, was a long console filled with computers and empty chairs. Brooks pivoted to the right and took his firing hand from his weapon to point at the far corner of the room. Sean followed his aim; at the end of another set of workspaces, a black chair tilted back with an arm coming out from the side and resting on the desk.

Brooks moved toward the chair on the toes of his feet. He hovered over the chair and smiled. Looking at Sean, he put a finger to his lips and waved Cloud into the room. Cloud proceeded in and let the door quietly shut behind him. Brooks reached down and violently spun the chair away from the console, the chair's sleeping occupant screeched and tried to stand. Before he could, Sean was already hovering over him, his barrel pressing into the man's chest.

The young, clean-shaven, and uniformed man's eyes searched the room in a panic then locked on Cloud.

"Colonel," he said. "You were reported as dead!"

"Yeah, well, I'm not. Where is the rest of the crew?" Cloud asked, moving to the bank of monitors, watching as camera views changed.

"Sir, there are only three of us on this watch now. I'm alone for another…" The man paused to look at a clock on the wall. He went to speak then paused and looked away. "Wait… who are these men?"

Sean brought the tip of his suppressor up and pressed it against the man's forehead. "We are asking the questions here," Sean said.

The man's hands rose from his sides. "Sir, I'll do whatever you want… just, please, when you leave, take me with you," he pleaded.

The sincerity of the man's tone caused Sean to back off, removing the barrel from his forehead. "That ain't very loyal to your cause, now is it?" Sean said.

The man looked up at Sean with wide eyes. "What cause? This place… there is nothing left here." He looked back to Cloud. "Sir, after you were reported dead, everyone started leaving, slipping out at night; some of the perimeter patrols just drove off. What security that is left is guarding the housing decks."

"Guarding from who?" Sean asked.

"Keeping them in," the man said. "The general has gone mad; we heard he attacked an Army base. Some of the contractors came back, but they took heavy losses and failed to do whatever they went out there after. The general went crazy over it. I'm telling you, sir, he's lost it; you gotta take me with you."

Cloud put up his hand and looked at the man's shirt, seeing his name. "Okay, Robinson, that's enough."

Sean looked at his wrist and checked his watch. "Sir, the locks?" he said.

Cloud looked at the monitors then back at Robinson. "I need you to open the blast doors."

"But, sir…" Robinson said.

Cloud walked to the chair and leaned over the man. "I need you to open the blast doors."

Robinson swallowed hard and pointed to the far consoles. "I can do it, but the alarms and strobes will sound; I can't override them," he said.

Cloud nodded. "Good, I want you to sound the evacuation alarm as well. Open every door, unlock every lift."

The man moved across the consoles. There was a large plastic case on hinges that he swiveled back and revealed three large metal dials and a number of switches. He looked back at Cloud. "Sir, I can open the blast gate, elevators, and doors and almost everything else except the lower levels."

Sean looked at Cloud. "What's down there?"

"The general and the laboratory," Cloud said. "Robinson, get the doors open, and then you're coming with us."

The man flipped the dials and toggled the switches, and then the loud tone sounded—high and low beeps. A strobe light above the door began to flash a blue LED light. Robinson walked to a wall where, encased in the concrete, was a metal door; he opened it, revealing a keypad just like the one over the entry door. The man pulled a card from out of his shirt, swiped it over the reader, and entered a series of numbers. The keypad began flashing red, and he entered another combination. The blue strobe over the door turned to red and the tones changed to a siren.

"It's done, sir," Robinson said. "That's the order to evacuate." The man walked to a center console to a phone that had already begun ringing. He grabbed the handset and ripped it from the wall. "With no answer to confirm or deny the alarm, they will have to comply with the evacuation."

Cloud grabbed the man by the shoulder and led him to the door. "Stay with us, do exactly what we say, and you'll be okay; stray from that and Chief Rogers will shoot you dead. Do you understand?"

Sean moved ahead. "Sir, let's cut him free now; we don't need him anymore."

Cloud shook his head. "We need him to get to the lower levels. The lifts at the end of the passageway require two keycards to enter; if we wait on the Rangers, all the lab work might be destroyed or moved."

Cloud did not wait for a response; he opened the door and stepped into the now brightly lit hallway. The evacuation alarm had activated all of the lighting. Bright light spilled over the whitewashed concrete walls. Doors opened in the corridors as uniformed men and women left rooms and stepped in the passageway with confused faces.

"Gas leak! Everyone out!" Cloud yelled as he ran past them, headed for the lifts.

Sean and Brooks ran to keep up with Cloud and Robinson as they ran deeper into the bunker complex. The hallways slowly became more and more populated with people who took no interest in their presence, most completely ignoring the armed, uniformed men running toward them. At the end of the corridor was a large row of elevator doors. The doors opened and more people rushed out, most in uniform but not all.

Cloud turned and followed a branch the led off to the right. The corridor was dark except for a faint light illuminating stainless steel doors at the end. "Those were the lifts to the upper living spaces; we need the secure lift to the lower level."

Cloud ran until he was right on top of two stainless steel doors recessed into the walls. He guided Robinson ahead to a card reader between the double sets of doors. The man nervously pulled the card attached to a lanyard from around his neck and swiped the keypad. Robinson entered his code, and the pad began flashing green. Before Cloud could do the same, the keypad froze solid and the lift began to buzz.

"Someone's coming up," Robinson said, backing away.

The doors clicked and slid open. Sean and the others found themselves looking into the faces of four men in black uniforms, M4s on tactical slings hanging to their front. Two more men in the back wore white lab coats and carried heavy black bags. Sean and Brooks brought up their weapons, examining the men. Without hesitation, one of the men in black jumped to the left, firing his rifle. As he moved, the rounds impacted the floor, bits of concrete exploding and splintering. Sean fired his own rifle as the rest of the men leveled their M4s and tried to fight.

Brooks leaned left and fired a short burst, taking down two guards quickly. Sean turned and shuffled to the right while draining his submachine gun into the corner of the lift, where he knew the first man had jumped. As Sean moved, he saw his rounds hit true, ripping through the guard's torso.

The last remaining guard dropped back against the back of the lift. He took one of the men in lab coats behind the neck and held a pistol to his head; the second lab worker dropped and cowered to the floor. "Back off… you know who this is, right? You want the cure, so you won't want him dead."

The man pushed forward, keeping the hostage in front of him, the pistol still pressed to the man's head. He turned the man to try to navigate away from Sean and out of the lift. Sean kept his weapon up. "Sorry, friend; I have no idea who that is," Sean said. He let his empty MP5 hang from its sling, drew his sidearm, and aimed it at the guard. "You have three seconds to drop your weapon." Sean let his index finger activate a laser. A bright red dot illuminated on the guard's forehead. "One, two." Sean pulled the trigger and a single suppressed round hit exactly where the red dot had rested. The man in black's head snapped back, and his body dropped to the floor.

Cloud rushed forward and pulled the hostage away. "Chief, this is Doctor Simmons, our lead in the Primal research." Cloud stepped away from the doctor and over the dead guard, lifting one of the black bags. "Is this it?" Cloud said.

The doctor nodded. "It's everything. Aziz is dead... Reynolds ordered him killed and took the digital copies; these are the backups and vaccine vials. These men were taking us to Reynolds' helicopter."

"Is he still down there?" Cloud asked.

"Yes, but we don't need him; the vaccine is in here," Simmons said, pointing at the bags.

Cloud looked up at the flashing red strobe light and blinked in its glare. He took in a deep breath and relaxed his shoulders. "Robinson, lead these men out. There's a battalion of Rangers that should be here by now; they'll get you to safety."

Sean reached into the lift, grabbed one of the black bags from the floor, and tossed it into the corridor. He moved into the lift and stood next to Cloud. He dropped the magazine on the MP5 and quickly reloaded it. Brooks moved past the others and went to join him. "No, you have to make sure the cure gets to Ericson," Sean said.

"Chief, I can do this alone," Cloud said.

"Just hit the button so we can get his over with," Sean said, pointing to the single backlit button on the wall of the lift.

Chapter 27.

He walked ahead following Cloud along the dark corridor. The air was different here, much cooler and more damp, musty with the odor of mildew. This part of the corridor was empty and dark, only the distant end lit with bright lights. Sean could see activity at the far end of the hall; men in black uniforms rushed back and forth, running from room to room.

"They are taking everything with them," Cloud said, watching the shadows that darted from one room to another, gathering bags on a large cart.

Sean kept his eyes trained ahead, his posture becoming tactical; his knees bent as he stalked forward through the dark, the MP5's stock finding its way into the pocket on his shoulder. "Where are they going with it?" Sean asked. "Would the general know we were coming?"

"Probably another hide site. There are more like this one; the general would know where they are and how to gain access. I'm sure he had his suspicions that this day would come."

"Would he be welcome there, will the other sites take him in?"

"With the cure and a private army… yes," Cloud answered.

Men at the end of the hall finished piling their loot on the large cart; they gathered around it, carrying their weapons on slings. They began pushing it toward the lift in Sean's direction. Sean dropped into the alcove of a doorway; Cloud fell in behind him, pushing close. "What's the play, Colonel; we could go back and disable the lift, trap them down here."

"No, can't risk it; this has to end here," Cloud said.

"There are a lot of 'em and I'm guessing they won't lie down like your boy upstairs," Sean said.

Cloud put his hand on Sean's shoulder, watching the cart move closer. "You can go, Chief… I got this."

"Yeah, doesn't work that way. Get ready to drop your NODs, sir." Sean let his weapon hang on the sling, backed deeper into the alcove, and removed two grenades from his vest. Taking one in each hand, he pulled the pins and looked back at Cloud. "We go fast and hard; this is going to get messy."

Cloud swallowed and nodded his head. "Just do it."

Sean looked around the corner; the cart was within fifty meters. He let the first grenade's spoon fly free then cooked it for a two count before tossing it down the hall. He then followed it up with the second, pulling back into the alcove just as the explosion ripped and echoed while throwing a thick cloud of concrete dust and smoke up the tunnel. Sean stepped back into the dark, leveled his suppressed MP5, and fired a quick burst, blasting out the florescent lights in the ceiling.

He pulled his optics down over his eyes and pulled Cloud out into the corridor. Men lay scattered on the floor; those who were not dead moved around coughing and tried to orient themselves in the dark. Sean illuminated them with the green laser from his weapon, firing quick shots in their bodies. He paused, scanning those that lay around the cart. "If it moves, kill it!"

Ahead, someone fired a tracer round that burned past him, the 5.56 gunfire extra loud in the confined space. Sean sidestepped to the right and ducked while firing a volley in the direction of the muzzle flash. They moved past an open door, and Sean turned, seeing movement inside. He grabbed Cloud, halting him, and snatched a grenade from the colonel's vest; he tossed it into the room and closed the door, the blast throwing it back open.

"Where is he?" Sean said. Taking aim at a man patrolling ahead with a flashlight, Sean fired a single shot to the man's chest—dropping him to the floor—then another round, killing him. Cloud fired more shots at men who were following the point man, hitting one, while Sean dropped the other two.

"We need to get moving; they are going to get smart on us soon," Sean said. "We won't be able to hold them all off if they coordinate."

Cloud ran ahead and turned into a break off the tunnel then cut again, moving to the left. Gunfire erupted behind them as the guards panic-fired into the dark where they thought Sean still lurked. Cloud halted Sean with a fist as he approached an open vault, a large box of paperwork keeping the door from shutting. Cloud pivoted and looked into a narrow hallway—the inner door was also ajar.

Sean followed close behind Cloud through the airlock and into a dimly lit command center. Sean looked at the large screens and maps hanging on the walls, rows of empty workstations, and powered-off flat-paneled monitors. "Damn, you all commanding a moon mission down here?" Sean asked.

Ignoring the comment, Cloud stayed ahead of him, keeping his weapon up. Sean frowned as he followed the colonel down the walkway leading along the back wall of the command center. At the end of the walkway on the left was a glass breakout room; light leaked out from the windows. Cloud moved away from the wall and closer to the consoles. The door to the breakout hung open; Cloud made a wide turn and stepped inside, Sean staying just behind him.

Cloud moved into the room and stopped at a large wooden conference table. Sean posted up in the doorway so he could both see inside and cover the walkway. At the end of the conference room, an old man in a partial Army dress uniform stood up and backed away from a bank of cabinets; his face showed shock as he looked at Cloud.

"You son of a bitch. I thought you were dead, James." The man clapped his hands while smiling; he took a step forward, stopping when Cloud raised the barrel of his weapon.

"Why did you do it? Why did you send them after the girl?" Cloud asked. "You have the cure; why couldn't it be enough?"

The general stopped and leaned over the head of the table. "You know why, James. It's like the thirteen colonies out there, all making decisions independent of one another. We cannot have everyone doing their own thing. We need something… something big to pull us all back together."

"So you would hold the cure and pick who lives and who dies?"

"No, but I could leverage it as currency. Influence decision-making, at least until we are all united again. It's the only way we survive, James. United, we stand… Divided, we fall."

Cloud lowered his head, shaking it. "It's over, sir."

The general stood, pounded his fists into the hardwood table, and shouted, "This isn't over; it's only the beginning!"

"We have Simmons, we have the research, and we have the girl. Colonel Ericson will be delivering it to Fort Sam Houston; he promises me we will distribute it globally as soon as possible. Once we stop the spread, we can begin the eradication of the infected. The nation's politics can work themselves out." Cloud lowered his weapon and dropped his head. "I'm done."

General Reynolds stepped away from the table and reached for his jacket hanging over a chair. "Dammit, Cloud, get back here. It's not too late; we can still fix this."

Cloud turned his back and walked to the door.

"We've come too far, done too much to quit now. James, don't you walk away from me!"

Reynolds pulled at his jacket, spinning his chair; a black 1911 became visible in a shoulder holster under the jacket. Sean spotted the weapon as the general took it in the palm of his hand. Sean stepped forward, taking aim and attempting to fire—Cloud was in his line of sight. Sean yelled a warning and dove forward, tackling Cloud, both men firing weapons as he fell.

Chapter 28.

Hassan smiled and embraced Brad in a long hug, letting go only to grab him by the shoulders and shake him. "We have much to talk about, my friend," Hassan said jovially. "I have a wife now; you must meet her. We can find you a wife as well."

Brad smiled back at the Afghan scout, looking beyond him to the large group of people moving down the trail toward the lake camp. "You did good, Hassan; you kept them all together."

"And you brought us here," Hassan said. "The fighting can end now."

As Dan promised, they were high in the mountains, far from any sign of Primals or bandits. Wood-sided buildings surrounded a large, clear, blue lake. A tall grassy field ran up the hillside meeting towering trees. The field could be used for farming, and Dan said the woods were full of game, so there would be no shortage of food.

"It'll be good here, Hassan. You can have a new start," Brad said.

"We can all have a new start." Hassan grinned. Looking over the land in deep thought, his gaze turned to the long column of people moving to the lake. "Yes, we will. Brad, I would like to see you tonight at the dinner fire," Hassan said, leaving to catch up with the others.

A man came up behind him and slapped an arm around his shoulder. "So, what do ya think?"

It was Turner; he pulled Brad in and watched as the others moved down the hill. Chelsea, Cole, and Mendez were taking baggage from the civilians; Henry was hovering over the children, helping them along. Joey stood on a large rock with Joe-Mac, stoically keeping watch over the procession of people.

"I think I might try to get home," Brad said. "I'm not sure if this is the right place for me."

Turner let go and dug through his shirt pocket for a cigarette. "I don't know, Thompson; this might be your home. I hear Bragg and Benning are a total loss."

Brad laughed and walked to a nearby tree to lean against it. "No, I mean my real home… Michigan. Cloud said there were still people up there; maybe my folks are still alive."

Turner lit the cigarette and watched the families move down the hill. "I heard what you said to Hassan… about a new start. You could do that here too. I see the way you look at that girl; maybe she's the one for you."

"I don't know," Brad said.

"Thompson, you can rest now, brother; it's okay to stop," Turner said. He took a long drag on the cigarette and walked away, leaving Brad alone.

Brad heard the thumping of a helicopter. He paused and searched the sky, watching as the civilians on the trail did the same. The Black Hawk circled around then landed near the base of the lake. The helicopter's engines shut down but the doors remained closed until the rotors stopped. Brad watched the doors open and Colonel Cloud step out. From somewhere near the cabins, a woman screamed and ran toward the helicopter, a young child chasing after her with Dan Cloud close behind them.

Brad sat against the tree watching the reunion. He then saw Brooks and Sean step out of the helicopter. They were introduced to Cloud's family and his father, Dan, before Cloud moved away, leaving Brooks and Sean sitting in the open door of the Blackhawk.

Brad stood silently watching the unfamiliar sight of smiling and happy people. Maybe this was a safe place for all of them. Maybe it could be his fresh start. He moved away from the tree and walked to the lake while searching the faces. He saw her; she was smiling and walking back up the hill toward him. She stopped to wave. Brad waved back, but it wasn't him she was looking at. Shane moved from the group, walking behind the others, holding Ella's hand. Chelsea ran forward and lifted Ella in a tight hug then grabbed Shane, embracing them all as a group... like a family.

"They deserve it," Brad said to himself.

Brad walked away, staying wide of the group and moving to the seated men at the helicopter. As he approached, Brooks tossed him a can of still cold beer.

"So this is why you all didn't leave to join the others?" Brad laughed.

Brooks moved over to allow Brad to sit in the helicopter's open door next to him. He handed Brad an already lit cigar. "Ericson gave us these as a going away gift."

Sean popped the top on a second beer, tossing an empty to the ground at his feet. "And I ain't about to share them."

Brooks reached for a leather bag the size of an eyeglass case and removed a small white cylinder. He took the tube and pressed it against Brad's thigh; a pop and hiss came from the tube.

"Ow! What the hell was that?" Brad said, pulling away and wincing while reaching down to rub his thigh.

Sean laughed. "Stop crying—it's another gift from Ericson; the vaccine, one of the first batches."

"Well, hell, you should have given it to one of them," Brad said, still rubbing his thigh.

"Yeah, thought you might say that; that's why you got the surprise pop." Brooks chuckled, draining his can and digging into the cooler behind him for another beer.

"So did they get him?" Brad asked. He opened his can and took a sip; he looked out at the lake, the water a deep blue.

"The general's gone. Ericson rounded up the survivors and moved everyone to Fort Sam Houston. They are starting a lab and plan to mass-produce the vaccine. If they can stop the spread, it won't be long before they develop a plan to contain the infected," Sean said.

Brooks slapped Brad on the back. "And just like that, we are suddenly unemployed."

Brad sipped at the can of cold beer, savoring the taste while watching his people gather around the shore of the lake. "They're going to be okay," he said.

"It's going to get boring here when the beer runs out," Sean said.

Brad tipped back his head, draining the can before crushing it and letting it fall to the ground. "You know where we could find some more?"

Coming Soon from
W.J. Lundy
The Shadows, Follow up to
The Darkness
FALL 2015

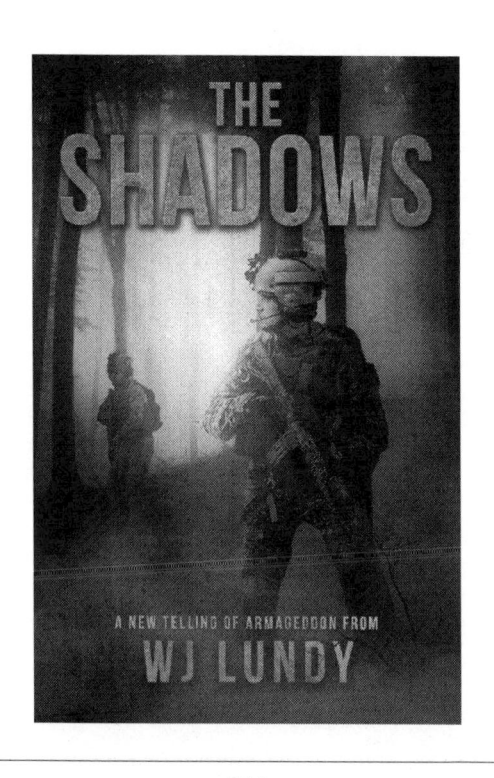

Thank You for Reading

If you have an opportunity Please leave a review on Amazon

Lundy W. J. (2015-08-01).

Whiskey Tango Foxtrot: Volume VI

W. J. Lundy is a still serving Veteran of the U.S. Military with service in Afghanistan. He has over 14 years of combined service with the Army and Navy in Europe, the Balkans and Southwest Asia. Visit him on Facebook for more.

OTHER WORKS BY WJ LUNDY

ESCAPING THE DEAD
W.J. LUNDY

TALES OF THE FORGOTTEN
W.J. LUNDY
A WHISKEY TANGO FOXTROT NOVEL

ONLY THE DEAD
LIVE FOREVER
W.J. LUNDY
WHISKEY TANGO FOXTROT

WALKING IN THE
SHADOW OF DEATH
A WHISKEY TANGO FOXTROT NOVEL
W.J. LUNDY

SOMETHING TO FIGHT FOR
A WHISKEY TANGO FOXTROT NOVEL
W.J. LUNDY

THE
DARKNESS
WJ LUNDY

OTHER AUTHORS UNDER THE SHIELD OF

SIXTH CYCLE

Nuclear war has destroyed human civilization.
Captain Jake Phillips wakes into a dangerous new world, where he finds the remaining fragments of the population living in a series of strongholds, connected across the country. Uneasy alliances have maintained their safety, but things are about to change. -- Discovery **leads to danger.** -- Skye Reed, a tracker from the Omega stronghold, uncovers a threat that could spell the end for their fragile society. With friends and enemies revealing truths about the past, she will need to decide who to trust. -- Sixth **Cycle** is a gritty post-apocalyptic story of survival and adventure.

Darren Wearmouth ~ Carl Sinclair

DEAD ISLAND: Operation Zulu

Ten years after the world was nearly brought to its knees by a zombie Armageddon, there is a race for the antidote! On a remote Caribbean island, surrounded by a horde of hungry living dead, a team of American and Australian commandos must rescue the Antidotes' scientist. Filled with zombies, guns, Russian bad guys, shady government types, serial killers and elevator muzak. Dead Island is an action packed blood soaked horror adventure.

Allen Gamboa

INVASION OF THE DEAD SERIES

This is the first book in a series of nine, about an ordinary bunch of friends, and their plight to survive an apocalypse in Australia. -- Deep beneath defense headquarters in the Australian Capital Territory, the last ranking Army chief and a brilliant scientist struggle with answers to the collapse of the world, and the aftermath of an unprecedented virus. Is it a natural mutation, or does the infection contain -- more sinister roots? -- One hundred and fifty miles away, five friends returning from a month-long camping trip slowly discover that death has swept through the country. What greets them in a gradual revelation is an enemy beyond compare. -- Armed with dwindling ammunition, the friends must overcome their disagreements, utilize their individual skills, and face unimaginable horrors as they battle to reach their hometown...

Owen Ballie

SPLINTER

For close to a thousand years they waited, waited for the old knowledge to fade away into the mists of myth. They waited for a re-birth of the time of legend for the time when demons ruled and man was the fodder upon which they fed. They waited for the time when the old gods die and something new was anxious to take their place. **A young couple was all that stood between humanity and annihilation**. Ill equipped and shocked by the horrors thrust upon them they would fight in the only way they knew how, tooth and nail. Would they be enough to prevent the creation of the feasting hordes? Were they alone able to stand against evil banished from hell? **Would the horsemen ride when humanity failed?** The earth would rue the day a splinter group set up shop in Cold Spring.

H. J. Harry

Printed in Great Britain
by Amazon